MW01103660

A GOOD YEAR
FOR MURDER

A GOOD YEAR FOR MURDER

by A. E. Eddenden

ACADEMY

CHICAGO

Published in 1988 and
Reprinted in 2000 by
Academy Chicago Publishers
363 West Erie Street
Chicago, IL 60610

Printed and bound in the U.S.A.

Library of Congress Cataloging-in-Publication Data

Eddenden, A. E.
   A good year for murder.

   I. Title.
PR9199.3.E32G66   1988   813'.54   87-35179
ISBN 0-89733-476-0

To MKI

FEBRUARY

Russia began a concentrated attack against her small neighbour, Finland. The younger generation hummed, or tried to imitate, Bonnie Baker's rendition of "Oh Johnny". Joe Louis successfully defended his heavyweight boxing crown with a unanimous decision over a little-known South American, Arturo Godoy. W. C. Fields, under the stage name of Cuthbert J. Twillie, traded insults and compliments with Mae West in the film, "My Little Chickadee". The number one radio star was Chase and Sanborn's hand-carved truant, Charlie McCarthy. And Mrs Gertrude Valentini, junior Alderman from ward six in Fort York, received a dead, unplucked chicken in an unmarked cardboard box. It was hand delivered on the fourteenth, St. Valentine's Day. Appropriately, the bird had an arrow through its heart. On opening the parcel, Mrs Valentini fainted.

All these items were reported by the city's influential, and only newspaper, *The Fort York Expositor.* The one about the chicken heart was allotted the smallest space (one column x ten agate lines) because it was really the least important item; except, of course, to Mrs Valentini.

MARCH

On St. Patrick's Day, Emmett O'Dell, also a politician, returned from a late council meeting to his home to find his pair of white toy poodles dyed a brilliant paddy green. The dogs were otherwise unharmed, even quite frisky, but, except for their eyes, were the colour of sunlit emeralds. They had been kept outside, as usual, in their elaborate doghouse (drapes and broadloom matched those in his wife's bedroom) and therefore relatively easy prey for a prankster.

The Fort York Expositor gave this item more space (two columns x twelve agate lines) partly because Mr O'Dell was a senior Alderman in his ward but also because his brother-in-law, who enjoyed embarrassing his wife's relatives, worked in the news department of the daily paper.

APRIL

April Fool's Day fell on a Monday. It was also the Mayor's birthday, a fact made much of by his opponents and detractors.

Phinneas 'Fireball' Trutt was an ordinary man for a mayor; medium height, spindly, uncoordinated arms and legs protruding from his round body, thick shock of white hair atop his red face, bulbous nose and always, his lower lip pushed out in a vacant expression that constantly seemed to ask, "What'll I do now?"

After twenty years as a professional fire fighter, he had entered the mayoralty race last election and surprised everyone, including himself, when, more through the incompetent campaign management of his rivals than Trutt's political wisdom, he slipped through the democratic check system into the highest seat on Fort York's Council.

Once he was sworn in, it was discovered, much to the enlightenment of City Hall society, that his shortcomings had obscured his strongest trait . . . a tactless, brutal honesty. Mayor Trutt had offended Council members, insulted visiting dignitaries, ruffled the feathers of almost every support group in the city and unwittingly set the stage for his April Fool's Day misadventure.

Because of his frank approach to all problems, it was no secret that the Mayor himself had a problem. He had an irrational, bowel-watering fear of fire. Whether he had joined the Fire Department many years ago to overcome this fear, or left to escape it, was not clear now even to him. But everyone knew about his phobia.

The intricate fire alarm system in his house, with the outside sirens and inside bells, had actually been the subject of a fifteen-minute local radio show. And at three o'clock in the morning of April 1, the system showed its merits. In less than a minute after it sounded, Mayor Trutt was out of bed, down the stairs and standing on his front sidewalk. The cooler heads in the family (his wife and children) smelling no smoke and seeing no flame, methodically searched the house while the Mayor, shivering in

3

the early-morning breeze, remained at a safe distance. His oldest boy, nineteen, who enjoyed a curiosity and mechanical aptitude that had skipped a generation, found a short circuit in the alarm system on the outside back wall. Swinging from the copper wire that had caused the trouble was a tiny doll, a jester. Its miniature, pliable fingers clutched a piece of white paper that bore the simple, printed message, "April Fool".

This time, *The Expositor* devoted a half page to the story, partly because it was about the Mayor, but mostly because an anonymous phone call was made to one of *The Expos*'s photographers shortly before the alarm went off. The story made both the early and late edition on April Fool's Day. And the picture was a good likeness, really. It showed that the Mayor slept in the raw. In fact, if he hadn't covered his private parts with the blue satin souvenir cushion of Their Royal Majesties' 1939 visit that he'd grabbed in his flight, the picture couldn't have been published at all.

Probably the most interested citizen of these events, other than the prankster, was Traffic Inspector Albert V. Tretheway* of the Fort York Police Department. He had read about the Valentine's Day chicken with great interest; the green poodle story had given him—to use his own vernacular—a twitch to his professional colon; and when Mayor Trutt became the official 1940 April Fool, Tretheway was convinced that this was more than a series of unrelated pranks.

"I almost expected this."

"Eh?" Jake, or really, Jonathan Small, Constable Second Class, shook himself from a snooze he was enjoying after another one of Addie's satisfying but heavy dinners. He sat up, cleared his throat, blinked and rubbed his eyes. "Expected what?"

"This Mayor Trutt thing."

"Oh?" Jake noticed that Tretheway was studying the late edition. "How about that picture?"

"God bless Their Majesties," Tretheway said.

They chuckled as conspirators with this new fuel to heap on the ever-smouldering fires of police/firemen rivalry. Jake stopped chuckling.

* pronounced Tre-*thew*-y

"You say you expected this?" he asked.

"Something like it."

"How come?"

"The other two could be a coincidence. Two unrelated happenings. But a third one makes it a series."

"You think there's some connection, then?"

"Bet my pension on it."

"Why?"

Tretheway shifted his bulk uncomfortably on his elbows and leaned forward in his oversized chair. Ashes rolled down his chest onto his stomach. He belched finally and settled back.

"Mrs Valentini. O'Dell. Mayor Trutt." Tretheway ticked the names off on his stubby fingers. "They're all politicians."

"That's true," Jake said.

"All the tricks took place on holidays."

"True again."

"And once a month, don't forget."

"What's that mean?"

"I don't know. But it's a pattern. Why didn't something happen on Ash Wednesday? That's a holiday."

"Maybe the prankster's religious."

"Maybe. But if it is a pattern, nothing more'll happen this month."

Jake, becoming interested, dug his wallet out of his back pocket. "Let's just check." He took out a small calendar. "April . . . Passover, Good Friday, Easter."

"I think we're safe for April."

"How about May?" Jake went on. "Mother's Day, Ascension, Queen's Birthday."

"That's the one."

"Eh?"

"The twenty-fourth of May. Queen Victoria's Birthday."

"How come?"

"It seems right," Tretheway said. "Firecracker Day. I think that would appeal to him."

"Him?"

"Or her."

"But the same person."

"Yes." Tretheway pulled deeply on his cigar. Then for a full minute he blew out what Jake called thinking smoke rings. Jake waited.

"There's a flair here," Tretheway said finally. "A showmanship. The same in all three. Almost a boastful trademark."

"You seem worried. He hasn't hurt anyone."

"No. Not so far." Tretheway heard Addie coming and quickly turned the newspaper picture of the exposed Mayor face down. Addie's entrance was announced by the rattle of fine china as she pushed the tea trolley across the hardwood floor of the dining room and onto the parlour rug.

"Tea time, gentlemen," she said.

Tretheway pushed himself up from his chair as he did whenever a lady entered the room, even his own sister, and Jake, rising also, once again marveled at the physical spectacle of his boss.

Tretheway's weight hovered between 280 and 340 pounds depending on the time of year. It was unevenly distributed over his 6'5", big-boned frame. His green eyes were squeezed beneath heavy, black brows, as black as his thick straight hair (not counting the greying sideburns he shaved off daily) and his oversized nose, surrounded by tiny blue crisscrossing veins, hung over a pair of almost invisible lips. When he smiled, or more likely grimaced, two rows of small ragged teeth appeared. From there, his ruddy clean-shaven chins folded usually into the black-braided collar of a senior officer's tunic. But in the comfort of his own parlour, they fell into the undone 'V' of his collarless regulation shirt. His chest was large, his stomach larger; his rear was wide and flat (a challenge to the police tailor) and his legs, muscular from years of competitive hammer throwing, ended in relatively small feet, size twelve. When he moved, the unlikely overall impression was a peculiar natural grace that sometimes comes with obesity.

Jake admired Tretheway. He envied him too, probably because he himself was bald, 5'8", 140 pounds and considered awkward unless he was driving. Jake looked from the Inspector to his sister. Adelaide Tretheway was slightly smaller than her brother, weighed slightly less and was much prettier, but at a distance, unfortunately, resembled Tretheway in a wig and a dress.

"Sit down, you two," Addie said in a voice that Jake regarded as pure music. "Here's your tea."

She handed Tretheway a large, full mug and gave Jake an ordinary cup and saucer. The tea was black and strong, the way Tretheway preferred, and by now Jake shuddered hardly at all when he swallowed it.

"Any treats?" Tretheway asked.

"Of course." Addie handed Tretheway a formidable slab of bright yellow cake slathered with icing.

"Jake?"

"Thanks, Addie." Jake accepted his piece, eyeing Tretheway's huge slice. Addie used to give her brother two normal pieces of cake until she discovered it embarrassed him.

"Now." Addie sat down and pulled her full skirt well over her knees to her large but what Jake considered well-turned ankles. "What about that prankster, Albert?"

Jake winced. In the five years he had been the Inspector's driver, assistant, boarder, and confidante (in that order) he had never heard anyone, except Addie, call Tretheway by his first name. His peers and superiors called him, simply, Tretheway and Jake used the titles Inspector, Sir, or Boss, depending on both their moods.

"You really should do something about it," Addie went on.

"Me?" Tretheway said. "What can I do?"

"Addie," Jake said. "When you get right down to it, all he's done is play a few tricks. Everybody's laughing about it."

"Well, maybe." Addie stirred her tea, spilling some into the saucer. "All the same, I'd feel better if he weren't out there . . . somewhere."

MAY

On the twenty-fourth of May, Firecracker Day, Tretheway's prophecies and Addie's fears were realized. Although not an earth-shattering event (the main news story was France defending her soil against her traditional German enemy), it was still more serious than the first three.

Between the Mayor and the eight city Aldermen, (two from each of four wards) was a supposedly unifying, guiding and exemplary body of three Controllers. William Lion MacCulla, Mac to his close friends, was the junior member of this board. The designation "junior" had nothing to do with age (MacCulla was thirty-six). It meant only that he had received fewer votes than the other two Controllers and more than the fourth, fifth, and sixth unsuccessful hopefuls who, in the last election, were two obscure communists and an interesting, lame-duck, write-in candidate named Herbert Drake. Mr Drake came fifth, or closest to MacCulla in the polls on the strength of a memorable slogan: "Even a Lame Duck Could Do Better". After the election it was discovered that Herbert Drake was an actual lame duck called Herby, which some Fort York University students had nursed back to health over a hard winter. MacCulla took it well enough (better than the communists) because he had graduated from the same University not long ago with a degree in European History.

Controller William Lion MacCulla was slight of frame and about the same height as Jake—5'8". His face was puffy, but pleasant. He affected rimless gold glasses which he constantly adjusted or polished. His fingernails were always clean. He was big in Boy Scouts, organized shopping or pleasure trips for older constituents and fought for more benches at bus stops. With this image, MacCulla captured the sympathy and votes of the over-sixty citizens of Fort York. In political circles, he was known as the old lady's darling and not too many of his colleagues took him seriously. From the top of his curly, greying hair to the tips of his small, elegantly pointed shoes, he exuded an old-school charm that had been fashionable in days gone by. He spoke with a lisp.

Controller MacCulla lived alone, halfway up Fort York's mountain (elevation 290') in a gracefully proportioned old house that had been remodelled into fashionable apartments. They boasted luxuries like ten-foot ceilings, thick sound-proof walls, silver leaf doors and deep fireplaces. It was the fireplace that caused the trouble.

At seven-thirty on the cool holiday evening, according to the police interrogation of a witness who was passing MacCulla's apartment at the time, there was a flash of light, an overlapping series of muffled explosions and a manly scream. The smoke poured out of an elegant ground floor casement window followed by Controller MacCulla who jumped the six feet to the grassy slope below. With his Scout uniform smouldering, he ran the quarter mile to the Emergency entrance of St. Joseph's Hospital in his stocking feet.

The hospital kept him for about two hours. They treated him for mild shock and second degree burns to his hands, left forearm and knees. His knees were scorched because of the inadequate protection provided by the regulation Scout shorts he was still wearing after the Victoria Day parade.

The firemen, called in by the same alert witness, had little to do in the way of fire-fighting. It was more of a housekeeping job. They swept up bits of blackened twigs, charred wood and small pieces of curly red paper. Most of the force of the explosion had been confined to the deep fireplace or immediately in front of the hearth. When MacCulla finally left the hospital in late evening, assisted by some of his concerned Scouts, he was greeted at his apartment by two Fort York detectives. They investigated and reconstructed the unfortunate event to the satisfaction of their superiors.

Because of the holiday, and some not unusual confusion in *The Fort York Expositor* news department, no reporters arrived until the next day, Saturday. So the story that the public read was a short, garbled version of the truth. It appeared in the special "Expo Flashes" box reserved for late-breaking local news and contained the adjective "mysterious" more than once—a tactic used by the newspaper's re-write men whenever they were short of space, facts or imagination. The full true story came out later that night in between euchre hands at the Tretheways'.

The Tretheway homestead was a large, solid brick three-story building on a quiet crescent in the west end of Fort York. Almost everything in the house was slightly oversized—bedrooms, verandahs, bathtubs, toilet seats, sunroom, cupboards, closets, root cellar—which suited the Tretheways admirably. It was a natural boardinghouse. And when Adelaide came from England to join her older brother Albert she recognized this immediately. They bought the house in 1923. It was considered an ambitious purchase for a young constable, but a thousand pound inheritance from a favourite aunt was more than enough to pay the down payment and remodel the house so that it could accommodate the economically necessary boarders.

Tretheway had second floor quarters of his own and so did Addie. This still left room for five or six boarders and, although there was a high natural turnover, there was seldom a vacancy. They were mostly Theology or Arts students, but in the last few years the number of uniformed boarders had increased.

Addie tried to make it their home and in most cases succeeded. Jake was the only more or less permanent guest; that is, he was the only one who wasn't going home from school or away to the war. And the social high point of the house (barring special occasions such as Christmas or New Years') was the Saturday night beer-drinking, cheese-eating euchre sessions. The boarders played for money, but the stakes were low. "Just enough to keep your mind from wandering," Tretheway used to say.

Tretheway and Jake, of course, were regulars. Addie played sometimes, usually when the students were away or studying for exams, and there were semi-regulars too: policemen friends, neighbours, or members of City Council, among others, who would come uninvited, but welcome, to take pot luck at the tables. One of the frequent contributors to the pot was Controller William Lion MacCulla.

"Can you hold the cards all right, Mac?" Addie asked. "Does it hurt?"

"Not bad, Addie." Mac plucked gingerly at his white gloves (an old pair he used to wear at official Scout functions) and noticed the burn ointment oozing through the thin material in several places. "I hope this guck doesn't get on the cards."

"They're old cards anyway," Addie said.

"There's some on mine." Tretheway had just been euchred for a two-point loss in a lone hand attempt. "Whose turn is it?"

Tonight there was only one table. Tretheway and Jake, traditional partners, were attacking Controller MacCulla and a Theology student boarder named Orlando Pitts.

"I think it's my deal," O. Pitts said.

O. Pitts, as he was always called, was an ordinary, run-of-the-mill apprentice minister. He didn't smoke, drink or make merry and frowned openly on people who did. But he was careful about Tretheway. Before taking lodgings, all Theology students were warned to resist their impulses to save the Inspector. Under no circumstances, Addie would tell them, were they to criticize his way of life, habits, language or character. She would place her large, soft hands firmly on the students' shoulders and, usually looking down at them, sum up by saying, "Inspector Tretheway is *not* to be considered your very own special challenge."

O. Pitts turned over a spade.

"Pick it up," Tretheway said. "I'll go it alone."

"Interesting." O. Pitts smiled.

Mac smiled too.

Jake put his cards face down on the table and coughed nervously. "Good luck, Boss."

Tretheway played his cards without hesitation, got a lucky trump split and took all the tricks—the last one, exuberantly, with the nine of hearts. O. Pitts' smile faded along with MacCulla's.

"Way to shoot, Boss," Jake said.

From the card table Tretheway brushed the cigar ashes that had fallen when he had played his last card.

"Mark up four, Jake."

He pulled all the cards together with his huge ruddy hands and, with surprising dexterity, shuffled them as expertly as any Monte Carlo dealer.

"We're six. They're four. One more lone hand'll do it, Jake."

He fired the cards accurately into four neat piles, one in front of each player.

"Lucky split," Mac grumbled.

"Nonsense," Tretheway said.

"I agree with Controller MacCulla," O. Pitts began. "The law of averages . . ."

"It doesn't much matter, does it, Sonny?" Tretheway bent toward O. Pitts. The table cut into his midsection. "We're still two points ahead."

"I know, but . . ."

"How are your drinks, gentlemen?" Addie rescued O. Pitts.

"I'm fine, Addie," Mac replied. Jake shook his head and put his hand up in polite protest, his mouth full of Shandy.

Tretheway, without speaking, held up an empty, 22-ounce bottle of Molson Blue. Addie, also without speaking, took it from him. "Tell us about yesterday, Mac," she said, on her way to the kitchen.

"That's right," Jake said. "The account in *The Expo* was pretty sketchy."

"There isn't much to tell, really," Mac began.

"Tell about what?" O. Pitts asked.

"MacCulla's accident yesterday," Jake said.

"Didn't you wonder how he hurt his hands?" Tretheway stared at O. Pitts.

"I've been studying," O. Pitts said.

"Go on, Mac." Addie was back at the table. She put Tretheway's full bottle of beer in front of him with, as usual, no glass. Tretheway's definition of an important dress-up affair was one in which beer was drunk from a glass.

"I'll tell you just what happened," Mac said. "But there isn't much."

He pushed his chair back from the table, crossed his thin legs and placed his hands awkwardly and gingerly in his lap. Addie rested her arm comfortably along the back of Jake's chair. Jake smiled up at her. Tretheway, pretending not to notice, rocked back on his special sturdy card-playing chair and folded his arms as far as they would go. Because of his chest expanse neither hand quite reached the other arm but came to rest, modestly, one on each breast.

"Remember last night was cool," MacCulla went on. "And rainy. I was really tired after the parade." He adjusted his glasses. "And cold. All I thought about on the way home was a nice warm fire. And maybe a warm toddy. I let myself in the apartment, folded my jacket, kicked off my wet shoes." He thought for a moment. "I pushed a window open a bit. Helps the fire draw. Struck a match. And threw it in the fireplace. That's about it. There was this big explosion. Then confusion, I guess. It scared me. And the pain. It's hard to remember. But I must've panicked. Jumped out the window and ran."

"How long between the time you threw the match and the explosion?" Tretheway asked.

"Maybe ten seconds."

"And what caused the explosion?"

"Firecrackers."

"Firecrackers," Tretheway repeated. "I should've known. On Firecracker Day. Still, seems like a lot of damage."

"They were giant cannon crackers. About ten of them all tied together. And the police said the fireplace directed the force of the explosion straight out. Right at me."

"Didn't you see them?"

"No. I usually make up the fire early. This one the night before. Paper, wood, kindling. All ready to go. Sometimes it's there for weeks. Nothing worse than an empty fireplace. The cannon crackers were hidden under the papers, I guess."

Tretheway unfolded his arms and leaned forward. "Then you're saying someone must've planted the crackers between the time you made up the fire late Thursday, and Friday night when it exploded?"

"Sounds reasonable. And I was out all day Friday."

"And your place was locked up?"

"Yes. But it wouldn't be too hard to break in."

"Any sign of forced entry?"

"Only when we came home from the hospital."

"We?"

"Some of my Scouts. They came to see me in the hospital."

"How did they know you were there?"

"They came to the apartment for a meeting. The firemen must've told them what happened."

"A meeting after a parade?"

"We always do. Go over anything that went wrong in the march. See if we can improve our procedure."

"Admirable. But you say there were signs of a break-in then?"

"I'll say. The firemen had broken the door down."

"Oh." Tretheway looked at Jake. "Axe-happy."

"Standard procedure," Jake said.

"Then, really, we still don't know who did it." Addie looked hopefully from face to face. "I mean, it could've been children. Just a prank."

"I don't think so, Addie," Tretheway said.

"Oh dear."

"Now, Addie," Jake said. "I know it's no joke having first degree burns," he looked sympathetically at Mac, "but it's hardly a case yet for the Crown Attorney. It could've been meant just to scare Mac. A prank like the others. But whoever did it simply miscalculated the force of the crackers."

"Oh dear," Addie said again. "And to think that Albert knew all along."

"What?" MacCulla straightened up and winced when his bandaged hands hit the table. Everyone turned to Tretheway.

"I didn't know," Tretheway protested.

"You predicted the day and the victim," Addie said, not backing down.

"You did?" Mac looked at Tretheway. "You picked Firecracker Day?"

"Lucky guess," Tretheway admitted.

"And me?"

"No, no. I said a politician."

"Still, I'm impressed." Mac leaned back in his chair.

"How about the next one, Boss?" Jake asked, half kidding.

Jake waited quietly for an answer. Mac's glass stopped halfway to his lips. O. Pitts stopped fidgeting. A girl student and two other boarders across the room stopped talking.

"I don't know," Tretheway said, finally. "I think I'll quit while I'm ahead."

Conversation resumed. Mac took a gulp of his drink. But Jake frowned.

"Aren't we going to play cards anymore?" O. Pitts whined. He had an unbeatable heart hand.

"Yes. For heaven's sake, let's change the subject," Addie said.

Tretheway turned the top card of the slush pile. It was the jack of spades. He picked it up.

"I'll go it alone, Jake."

Later in the evening, Jake had a chance to talk to Tretheway alone. It was the custom, mid-way through the card game, for Addie to interrupt with a large plate of giant-sized, old-cheese

sandwiches and tea, if anybody wanted it. She felt it gave everybody a needed break from the cards and drinking.

Tretheway took advantage of the break to shovel some more
coal into the furnace on this unseasonably cool May evening.
Jake followed him down to the cellar ostensibly to see if he could
help.

"Can I do anything?" he asked.

"Put some water in the humidifier."

"Right." Jake filled an old milk bottle from the stationary tubs
and walked around the back of the metal octopus that kept the
house warm. The water gurgled satisfyingly out of the bottle as
he tipped it into the opening. "Why didn't you . . . you know
. . . earlier?"

"Make another prediction?"

"Yes."

"Two reasons." Tretheway slammed the hot metal door shut
with the end of his shovel. "One. Everybody was listening. I had
the feeling that everyone was waiting for the pearls of wisdom to
fall. Or the great oracle to speak. They're putting too much importance on what I might say."

Jake nodded. "What about the second reason?"

"That's easy. There's only one holiday next month."

"Eh?"

"Check your calendar. Father's Day. The sixteenth."

"No others?"

"Not really. There's St. John the Baptist Day. But nobody cel-
ebrates that here. Nope. Father's Day. Has to be it."

"What do you think will happen?"

Tretheway leaned his shovel up against a concrete lock pillar.
"I don't know. This firecracker thing doesn't fit the pattern."

"I thought it did."

Tretheway shook his head.

"Among other things, how did anyone know for sure Mac would
light his fire on the twenty-fourth of May?"

Jake thought for a moment. "Took a chance?"

"Maybe." Tretheway shrugged.

"You have other reasons?"

Tretheway slowly blew a cloud of cigar smoke over Jake's head.
"Hell!" He slapped Jake on the back. "Let's go have some beer
and euchre."

JUNE

Father Cosentino had begun his ecclesiastical career as a Roman Catholic priest. Shortly before the Great War (WWI), he gathered together his savings, his belongings, the courage of his re-thought convictions and quit the legitimate church to join a less demanding religious sect. He still wore a black suit and shoes, still played golf on weekday mornings and retained the title of Father. But under the new regime, Father Cosentino was free to pursue other, more adventurous, avenues of life such as business, girls, horses, and politics. At the time of his defection, he ran for Fort York Board of Control and, to the surprise of the RC population, won handily.

In his ensuing successful political career (he never lost an election), he blessed everything from tug boat launchings to scissors at ribbon-cutting ceremonies. He said grace at most official dinners and led the city hall staff in Christmas carols and Easter hymns. It was not surprising that he became the official Chaplain for the City of Fort York.

As an Italo-Canadian, he openly criticized Mussolini in his early association with "those heinous, heartless animals called Nazis". And when The War began, his round, happy face was a common sight at rallies exhorting people to buy bonds or collect scrap paper. In gossipy circles it was said that he perhaps drank a little too much ceremonial wine, but this was a small fault beside his willingness to work for worthwhile causes.

Father Cosentino fought for underprivileged children, struck out fearlessly against all kinds of bigotry and attacked the maltreatment of birds and animals. He was a man with few, if any, enemies. All this made his murder hard to understand.

At first light on Sunday, June 16, Father Cosentino was discovered sitting stiffly upright in the open rumble seat of his recently acquired '35 Willys. On his lap was an open, empty gift box lined with tissue paper. An attached tag carried the handwritten greeting—"Happy Father's Day". Around the Father's neck was a new, four-in-hand tie, tied much too tightly, that hung, surely by accident, in the same sympathetic curve and coloured the same hideous purple as the priest's lolling tongue. And his eyes bulged.

A Patrol Sergeant on an old bicycle, checking the rounds of his beat Constables, turned in the alarm from a nearby call box when he first saw Father Cosentino sitting conspicuously in his car—the only car in the church parking lot. There was no one present in the warm, still morning, not even (according to the Sergeant's report) a cat or dog.

The first to answer the summons was Detective Sergeant Wan Ho. Born and raised in Fort York's small Chinatown and given the English Christian name of Charles long before Charlie Chan was created, Charlie Wan Ho had risen in quick succession from top police cadet to First Class Constable to Detective to Detective Sergeant. For the last ten years, he had been passed over for promotion because of his Chinese ancestry. Whenever a situation called for a high-ranking plainclothesman, as it did now, Police Chief Horace Zulp considered himself more suitable.

The Chief arrived late and took charge. He ordered the uniformed men to cordon off the area, which Wan Ho had already done.

"Sharp eyes, watch out. Suspicious characters. On your toes." He shouted instructions and encouragement. The detectives pounded on doors, waking sleeping residents and dogs, but received for their trouble mostly yawning heavy-lidded answers that didn't help at all. And Mayor Trutt's arrival was preceded by the sound of his personal ear-splitting siren waking the householders whom the door-thumping detectives had missed.

In cases as serious as this (homicides, air raid drills, strikes, large fires) all senior officers were called in regardless of department. By the time Tretheway and Jake got there in Jake's '33 straight eight black Pontiac convertible (they had taken the time to put on uniforms but not to pick up a cruiser) the crowd had grown. Newsmen, photographers, some early-shift steel workers and several locals added to the busy scene.

When Sunday was over, the policemen, firemen, news fraternity, neighbourhood and onlookers knew of the Father Cosentino murder. Monday evening, those citizens who had missed the news broadcasts on the Fort York radio stations were informed of the dastardly crime by *The Fort York Expositor.*

The facts of the murder were eventually run to earth. Several ties of identical design were found on the counters of Woolworths'. No employees were found who remembered a sale. It was concluded that the box (a common type very popular this Father's Day), the tie and the wrappings had probably been shoplifted. The handwriting was not identified. There were no footprints on the hard-surfaced parking lot. The car was clean of fingerprints—wiped clean. Nobody had heard or seen anything unusual.

Father Cosentino had been last seen by a neighbour on Saturday evening. The neighbour, also a parishioner, had a clear view of the church and the Father's adjoining apartment from her rear window. She had seen the good priest come out onto his back porch, presumably for a breather, while writing his sermon for the morning. "It was what he always did," she told the police. She usually waved at him, which she had done that night, and he had waved back in a friendly enough way before going inside.

The neighbour had then returned to her own living room to catch The Old Ranger on the radio telling another Tale of Death Valley Days. It started at nine-thirty. At eleven, when she had gone to bed, the pattern of lights at the church and at the Father's apartment had been normal.

Apparently, between midnight and five a.m., somebody had inveigled, forced, or tricked Father Cosentino out into the parking lot and into the rumble seat of his own car. As to what happened next, everyone had his own uncomfortable, imaginative vision. Particularly after what Dr Nooner said at the scene.

"There are bruises on both arms." Francis Nooner, M.D., was an outspoken, overweight physician who had successfully sought the post of Police Doctor because he hated late nights, house calls, office hours and regular patients. He played euchre at Tretheways' occasionally.

"Both forearms and wrists have a pattern of bruises that suggests the arms were held firmly . . ." The Doctor stopped when he saw the puzzled look on Tretheway's face. "You have a question, Inspector?"

"How could one man do that and . . .?"

"Hell. There was more than one."

Tretheway felt the hackles rising on his neck. "You mean we're after two . . .?"

"One on each arm, I figure. Another to strangle. Maybe one gagged him. There was lint in his mouth." Jake paled.

"Altogether, I make it three. Maybe four," the Doctor concluded.

THE COUNCIL MEETING
(Still June)

The governing body of the City of Fort York did what all sensible elected officials do in a crisis. They called a meeting.

On Tuesday morning, politicians, various minor civil servants, the City Clerk, many, many policemen and a sprinkling of spectators filled the Council chamber. Because the old meeting room had been designed for fewer people, the gathering had a misleadingly cosy aura. Talk hummed gaily. The morning air was still fresh and clean. Everyone smelled of perfumed soap or shaving cream. The pleasantly raucous sounds of the outdoor Farmer's Market next to the City Hall filtered up through the open windows.

As you entered the chamber, you faced the open end of an ingenious, horseshoe-shaped, three-tiered platform designed by the Fort York City Engineering Department. On the lowest tier, slightly above floor level, were eight desks for the eight Aldermen. At the rear of the horseshoe, a full six feet up and at dead centre, was the Mayor's chair. There was a round stained-glass window at about the Mayor's head level.

Approximately twenty-five hand-picked policemen filled the bottom three-quarters of the gallery that rose steeply, like some ancient surgeon's theatre, behind the Council's platform. In the row nearest the ceiling was the press gallery. Today it held two reporters from the Fort York radio stations, the regular police reporter from *The Expositor,* and, sitting apart, a Canadian Broadcasting Corporation journalist from the much larger, rival city of Toronto. Or Hogtown, as every loyal Fort Yorker called it. And, in retaliation, Torontonians called Fort York, Fart Yark.

At floor level within the 'U' of the horseshoe, among pieces of slightly smaller-than-normal office furniture, a number of civil servants arranged writing paper, sharpened pencils, filled ink wells and generally bustled about. Henry Plain, the City Clerk, sat at their centre. Henry had held this post for eighteen years and enjoyed it, despite the fact that he complained constantly about

being smothered in paper work. He was quick mentally and physically and recognized as an expert in parliamentary procedure.
His confident blue eyes had stared down many a fledgling Alderman over a point of order. And his creamy complexion, finely
chiselled features and well-groomed curly hair would not have
been out of place on a Hollywood movie stage. Unfortunately,
Henry Plain was five-foot-four with lifts. Oddly enough, none of
his staff was over five-foot-four. There was a rumour, started by
Mayor Trutt's detractors, that City Council would hire no one any
taller because of the expensive small furniture the Mayor had
had custom-made to fit the scheme of things.

Mayor Phinneas Trutt adjusted the magnificent chain of office
hanging around his neck. He rapped his gavel politely. "Order.
Ladies and gentlemen. Please."

The noise level lowered. As if at a hidden signal, everyone rose
and broke into an unaccompanied version of "God Save the King"
followed immediately by the Lord's Prayer. Everyone sat down.

"As this is a special—nay, emergency—meeting, I think we
can dispense with unnecessary details, such as new business,
minutes of the last meeting, etc. etc." Mayor Trutt pushed his
lower lip in and out. "The first thing we should do is pay our
respects to the departed Father Cosentino." He stood up. "If we
could all stand and face his desk for a moment's silence."

The chairs scraped back. Everyone in the room stood again
and faced the Controller's empty chair, now dramatically leaned
forward against his desk. The noise of shuffling feet and creaking
floors gradually subsided into a silence broken only by a few
muffled coughs and throat-clearings. Outside sounds, unnoticed
before, intruded: a traffic policeman's whistle, a siren, a blind
beggar's violin, a clanging streetcar bell.

"Thank you," the Mayor said quietly. "The funeral's at two
o'clock. That should give us enough time to finish this meeting
and have a nourishing lunch." He patted his stomach with both
hands. "Please sit down." The shuffling and creaking ended for
the second time. "Now it's time to turn the meeting over to him
in whose hands our lives are placed. Chief Horace Zulp."

The Council twisted awkwardly around in their seats to face
the Chief. Chief Zulp handed his notes to one of the Deputies
sitting beside him. From his front row seat in the gallery, he
stretched to his full height of almost six feet, clasped his working-

class hands behind his back and, rising up and down on the balls of his feet while staring at the ceiling (an attention-getting trick passed on to him by his evangelist father) waited for his audience to become quiet. It did. In a deep, gravelly voice (also passed on from his father) Zulp launched into an eye-glazing discourse on the Cosentino murder.

Chief Zulp was an old line policeman, twenty years Tretheway's senior in age and service. He had learned the rudiments of peace-keeping at a time when it was acceptable practice to put marbles in the fingers of your uniform gloves for flicking street urchins over the head. The Chief had a strong, athletic build. He had actually enjoyed a short career as a second string right wing for the Fort York Tagger Football Club. And although slightly over-weight, he was in reasonable physical shape for a man his age. His head was too large for his body, and his ears and nose were too large for his head. The deep furrows and lines that criss-crossed his face gave him an interesting, weathered appearance. Most new men were fascinated by the movements of his nose and jowls when he spoke. Even Tretheway found himself staring at the loose, wrinkled folds of skin rippling around Zulp's neck when he groped for the proper word or phrase. Chief Zulp enunciated concisely, but expressed himself mostly in short, ungrammatical bursts of information.

"So we're after a religious fanatic. My opinion. Strong. Very muscular. A lone strangler." Zulp rose up and down on the balls of his feet again. "Questions?"

"Sir!" Tretheway stood up.

"What is it, Tretheway?" Zulp snapped. He hadn't expected a question from one of his own men.

"On Sunday, at the scene of the murder, Dr Nooner, the police medical . . ."

"I know who he is, Tretheway."

"He suggested that there were at least three, maybe four as-sailants . . ."

"Nonsense!"

"Sir?"

The Doctor had, years ago, in his abrasive bedside manner, quickly and correctly diagnosed one of Zulp's heart attacks as gas. "He's no investigator," Zulp said. "Not trained."

"He mentioned bruises on the arms of the deceased."

"Could've come from anything. A fall, maybe. Or something."

"But Dr Nooner said . . ."

"Tretheway." Zulp smiled and spoke slowly as though to a child who couldn't grasp his multiplication tables. "If you cut your finger. Or break a bone. Or get scarlet fever. Then by all means, listen to the Doctor. Sensible. But remember. He's no policeman. But we are." He pointed at Tretheway. "Inspector." He pointed at his own chest. "Chief."

Tretheway sat down.

"More questions?"

Gertrude Valentini raised her hand.

"Mrs Valentini?" Zulp said.

"What are you going to do about us? About our protection." Although Alderman Valentini was perversely proud that she had been the first victim, she still shivered when she thought of the unknown and now murderous hands that had packaged her unusual St. Valentine's Day gift. "He could strike at any time."

"Alderman Valentini." Zulp smiled. "Glad you asked."

He nudged one of his Deputies who dove into a bulging briefcase and handed him a sealed envelope with the official Fort York coat of arms embossed in the corner.

"Thank you." Zulp made a small ceremony of opening the envelope. He pulled out a sheaf of letterheads—with the official crest again, this time accompanied by the heading "From the Office of Chief Constable"—and waved them reassuringly to the throng. "The Master Plan."

The Master Plan was simply a list of the Fort York Aldermen, Controllers and Mayor. Beside each was the name and rank of the two policemen who would guard each politician day and night. That was all there was to it. The junior Aldermen were assigned Constables. Senior Aldermen were guarded by Sergeants (ward four naturally had a Matron) while Controllers had Inspectors and their assistants watching over them. The Mayor, of course, was protected by the two Deputy Chiefs, except for official functions, parties, celebrations, etc., when Chief Zulp himself took over. Henry Plain had given Zulp a minor problem. Although Henry Plain was the unqualified ruler of the civil servants, he stood at the bottom of the political pecking system and, therefore, was an unlikely but possible victim. Zulp finally decided to allocate him two crossing guards from nine to five.

After a brief explanation of the plan, Zulp jumped right into the mechanics.

"Now. I'll call names. Aldermen first. Ward one. They'll stand up. The four policemen assigned to that ward will descend to the Council floor. Take up positions. Behind their respective charges." He turned and faced the rows of navy blue uniforms behind. "You've got your orders."

This explained the mysterious notes given to the policemen before the meeting. In the case of Tretheway and Jake, it contained one word: "MacCulla".

"Familiarize yourself with your man. Or woman. Make sure they know who you are. Introduce yourself. Shake hands if necessary." Zulp turned back to the meeting. "I'll continue through the Aldermen. Wards one to four. Then the Controllers. The Mayor." He thumbed through his pages for the proper sheet. "Now. Everybody ready?" Zulp, expecting no answer, paused only briefly. "Ward one. Alderman Lucifer Taz. And Alderman Morgan Morgan."

The two Aldermen rose. At least, Alderman Morgan rose. Lucifer Taz unfolded from his seat.

Taz was tall, very thin and appeared to be made up mostly of joints. His straight, black hair, plastered wetly against his forehead, and his equally black moustache accentuated the whiteness of his complexion. A scarlet boutonniere blazed tastefully against the drabness of his dark grey lapel. People often said that Taz looked like the perfect Funeral Director (which he was). Compassionate, discreet and knowledgeable in the ways of embalming and bereavement, he had made a deserved success of the undertaking business, in spite of his drinking.

As a politician, he was conscientious, dedicated, at times naïve, but always industrious. He put in more hours than necessary for his constituents. Taz had the best attendance record on Council. When he spoke at a meeting, his choice of words and syntax reflected a university education. His voice was higher than the average woman's.

Taz lived alone above the funeral home where, after work, he wore heavy red flannel or plaid shirts and stuffed his denim overalls into scuffed, hi-cut boots. In the outdoors (he took several church-sponsored camping trips a year) he wore a Hudson's Bay coat with a bonhomme togue and carried a rifle or paddle. He loved outdoor sports with a passion but could never summon the proper control to coordinate his ungainly length. Lucifer Taz was an enthusiastic, but incompetent, skier, snowshoer, hunter, and canoeist.

Alderman Morgan also drank. He had been born in India to Colonel and Lady Archibald Humphrey, who had given him the Christian name of Morgan, his mother's maiden name.

When young Morgan Humphrey was five years old, his father took part and was killed in a military action now remembered only by dusty English historians: The storming of Kabul, 1879. Morgan's mother went home to England and, never one to indulge in self-pity, remarried within six months. Her second husband was a close cousin with, unfortunately, the surname of Morgan. After many bitter discussions between the Morgans and the Humphreys, the new couple legally adopted the child, thus officially changing his last name to theirs.

Morgan Morgan, although now a Canadian and Fort York Alderman, still looked like a son of Colonel Archibald Humphrey. Morgan stood as though he were on parade, wore his clothes like uniforms and sported a military-style grey moustache. His language was surprisingly foul, but his cultured accent could only have come from years spent in a public (private) school.

The bond between Morgan Morgan and Lucifer Taz was alcohol. Whether together or alone, they drank gin and tomato juice in the morning, wine with their lunch, cocktails and brandy at dinnertime and finished each day with beer. Their attitudes towards drink differed. Where Taz gulped his like medicine with a scowl and shudder, Morgan, who outdrank Taz two to one, sipped his like fine wine, as though he were tasting it anew with each drink. The two were seldom completely sober. And the two policemen who joined the affable Morgan and Taz were specially chosen abstainers.

They mumbled introductions and then stood at ease in the small space behind the Aldermen's chairs. Taz and Morgan sat down.

"Good. Well done. Yes." Chief Zulp continued with the Master Plan. "Ward two. Alderman Emmett O'Dell. And Alderman F. McKnight Wakeley; Captain, stroke, Major-General."

The ward two Aldermen stood up. Wakeley saluted while O'Dell, the bigger of the two, smiled indulgently at the crowd who, he thought, had yet to live through anything like what he had lived through with his two bright green poodles.

Emmett O'Dell was a big man, slightly overweight, with a strong chin, sparkling eyes, large, wet teeth and shamefully curly little boy hair. He spoke in a lilting Irish brogue that called up visions of clay pipes, leprechauns, green fields and shamrocks. When he delivered a speech in Council, his voice was a formidable weapon.

Alderman O'Dell had been brought up in an atmosphere of green beer and maudlin Irish songs. He had been subjected to discussions, magic lantern slides, anecdotes and family histories that praised the Emerald Isle. But he had never been to Ireland. His ward, which contained Corktown, didn't know this.

The Alderman's present wife kept his secret. In fact, the two regularly exchanged presents on March seventeenth. This year, she had given him a too-tight green sleeveless sweater covered with small white harps.

Alderman F. McKnight Wakeley held his salute until the two policemen for ward two mounted the dais. He had this thing about saluting, or really about anything military.

Wakeley had joined the Royal Fort York Light Infantry (Reserve) in 1919 as an officer and worked his way up to Captain. He had also volunteered for the thankless position of titular head of a local high school cadet corps that was affiliated with the RFYLI. This gave him the official privilege of holding the rank of Major-General (Cadet). Although his reserve unit met only once a week, spent an annual ten days at summer camp and received a small stipend (usually free street car tickets) it still gave him the right to wear the King's uniform. This he did often. His favourite walk was from the City Hall to the armouries and back, returning salutes.

Alderman F. McKnight Wakeley was a past president of the Fort York District Officers' Institute (no women allowed), a social club for the military where battles were courageously re-fought over glasses of Pimms' Cups' #2, and brave stories of VC winners were re-told against the background of clicking billiard balls. He drank only socially, watched his diet and did calisthenics every morning to keep fit—which he was. His picture appeared in the foreground of a recruiting poster for the RFYLI. He was saluting.

"Ward three," Zulp continued.

Tretheway nudged Jake. The Tretheway boardinghouse was in ward three.

"Alderman Harold Ammerman, and Alderman Bartholomew Gum."

At the age of seventy-four, Harold Ammerman was the oldest member of City Council. He still had most of his wits about him, but forgot more appointments now and repeated himself more often than he had when he was younger. When interrupting, he had the habit of starting sentences with the annoying phrase, "If I might interject here".

Alderman Ammerman took his job seriously. As head of the Ward Three Recreational Committee, he worked long hours for the Children's Garden Program. On any clement Saturday morning, Ammerman could be seen gardening alongside groups of small children. He enjoyed an understanding and rapport with them that only the very old can share with the very young. Ammerman was ingenuous, easy going, quick to laugh and generous.

Alderman Bartholomew Gum shared some of Ammerman's attractive traits. He, too, was forthright, laughed loudly (if vacantly at times) and generally gave the impression of contentment with his lot.

Gum, forty-four years old, had lived in the same west-end house all his life and had supported his parents for the last fifteen years. What companions he had had in early life had married, moved away or just outgrown him. Bartholomew's best friend, after his mother, was his bicycle—a black one.

As a young Cub Scout, then Scout and now Scout Leader, Gum was familiar with every stone and tree in his nearby, beloved Coote's Paradise. He knew which trails led to the marsh or to the University, which ones doubled back on themselves or dead-ended and which ones led to the secret places where young, adventurous public school boys smoked their first dried hollyhocks.

Unlike Ammerman, Gum had a small, serious mouth, a button nose and fair, all but invisible, eyebrows and eyelashes. His thick hair was naturally curly and unnaturally jet black. And his weak, colourless eyes had peered through rimless spectacles since he was in the third grade.

Whenever Gum and Ammerman spent any time together, they laughed and talked jovially but seldom exchanged ideas or clearly understood each other.

Their bodyguards added to the congestion.

"Ward four," Zulp persisted. His voice softened condescendingly. "Alderman Gertrude Valentini. Alderman Ingird Tommerup."

The two women Aldermen perked up but remained seated. It was unusual, even in wartime, to have two ladies elected in a heavy-industry ward. But there were reasons.

Alderman Gertrude Valentini, a widow now for the last ten years, was a Canadian girl who, in a wild romantic youthful episode had fallen in love with and married a Sicilian. The late Mr Valentini had left her, among other things, a surname worth at least a thousand votes in the predominantly Italian ward six.

Gertrude Valentini was everyone's idea of a mother, and she was one. Her son, Gregory, was serving in the Atlantic Squadron of the Royal Canadian Navy. She had a becoming, sexless smile, a comfortable round body and bosom, a penchant for fainting and a wardrobe in which, somehow, everything resembled an apron. Her eyesight was poor. When time or privacy permitted, she would ferret out an old-fashioned lorgnette from her knitting bag to read the phone book or clarify a distant scene. She crocheted uneven antimacassars during Council meetings.

Mrs Valentini lived in a small four-room bungalow with lace curtains and a white picket fence. It was close to the factories. The fence was painted four times a year, at no charge, by the public relations department of a giant steel mill.

One of the other things her husband had left her was a secret formula for making odourless gin from rutabagas. Alderman Valentini drank a six-ounce tumbler of neat gin at bedtime and had a large smash every morning before breakfast.

Alderman Ingird Tommerup was the senior Alderman from ward four and looked every part of it. She was taller, louder, and huskier than Mrs Valentini. Her hair, as yellow and thick as her Viking ancestors', was always braided and either wrapped around her head or hung in girlish pigtails to her waist. She seldom wore a hat. Her big-boned frame was usually clothed in a mannish but expensively tailored suit. If necessary, she could out-ski, out-sprint, and out-folk-dance any man on Council.

Miss Tommerup had the confidence that comes with generations of wealth. Her father was the President and largest stockholder of STELFY—Steel Company of Fort York—the same company that painted Mrs Valentini's fence. He had used his power and wide influence to gain a seat for his only daughter on Council. "It's nice," he used to say, "to have a friend at City Hall."

Ingird lived mainly at home, but maintained a secluded cottage in the small, neighbouring village of Wellington Square for those days and weekends when she wished to get away from it all and literally let her hair down. Every morning before she left for City Hall, Ingird Tommerup shaved her upper lip.

The two police matrons assigned to ward four touched their white-gloved fingers to their foreheads and curtsied self-consciously to the lady Aldermen before pushing in behind their chairs.

Chief Zulp shuffled his papers importantly, looking for phase two of the Master Plan.

"Fair crowd down there, Jake," Tretheway observed.

"Building up," Jake confirmed.

"You suppose he's there?"

"Who?"

"The one who murdered Father Cosentino."

"Eh?" Jake sat up straighter.

"And killed Mrs Valentini's chicken."

"You think he's down there?"

"Just making conversation."

"What about Nooner's theory? There's more than one?"

"Could still fit in."

"You mean they're all down there?"

Tretheway abruptly changed the subject. "God, it's hot." He jammed his fingers in between his collar and bulging red neck, to let cool air in and hot air out.

Chief Zulp, as usual, had dragged the meeting out longer than expected. During this time, the temperature had risen and the humidity had increased. The inadequate ventilating system—two small, portable fans—did little to lessen the discomfort of the policemen and politicians who were being packed together on the platform.

Zulp cleared his throat noisily. He had found phase two of the Master Plan.

"And now for the Controllers," Zulp began.

"Controller MacCulla. And Controller Joseph L. Pennylegion."

Tretheway pushed himself up again and, accompanied by Jake and two other policemen of suitable rank, walked down the steep gallery steps. They climbed onto the dais. With Tretheway leading the way, he and Jake gingerly twisted around and side-stepped people on the way to their assigned positions behind MacCulla.

"Jake," Tretheway observed, "this platform doesn't feel safe."

"I know," Jake answered. "Just tread lightly."

"What do you mean by that?"

"Nothing. Everybody should just walk easy. That's all. Hi, Mac."

"Hi, Jake. Tretheway." Mac pantomimed wiping his brow and panting. "Pretty hot, eh? Got enough room back there?"

"No," Tretheway said. "Pull your chair in."

"It is in."

"I'm too close to the edge."

"Me too," Jake said.

"I'm sorry," Mac said. "You'll just have to squeeze in more."

As Tretheway eased his way sideways into the safety valve of space left respectfully around Controller Father Cosentino's chair, he noticed his and Jake's counterpart squeezing behind the chair of the Senior Controller.

Joseph L. Pennylegion's smoothly run and financially well-oiled political machine had managed to get him the lion's share of the votes for Board of Control. This made him, politically, second only to the Mayor. If for any reason Mayor Trutt was unavailable—sickness, vacation, death, etc.—Controller Pennylegion officially headed the City of Fort York as its acting Mayor. This situation frightened most of the Council members.

Although Pennylegion had no known police record, he had the aura or mystique of the successful criminal. His chauffeured car was a black eight-passenger Packard rumoured to be bulletproof. Strange people had been seen dropping into his fashionable mansion at odd hours. His friends, strangers to most of the Council, appeared and disappeared mysteriously without being introduced. And they had names like Quick Roy, Crowbar, Salamander, Dink, and The Beak. "Old buddies," Pennylegion would say when forced into an answer, "from the car days."

True, he had been in the car business—more used trucks, really. It was said that he had made his fortune selling specially equipped trucks to the bootlegging fraternity during American Prohibition. But, as Tretheway said in defence of the judiciary system, if hearsay evidence was acceptable in court, most City Council chambers would be empty.

Controller Joseph Pennylegion was a big man, too heavy, with flaming red hair and a temper to match. He was loud in voice and dress, offensive to well-brought-up ladies, and a compulsive gambler.

On the plus side, he was neat. His hair was always waveset into place, his clothes and fingernails always clean. He took two baths a day and smelled of cologne. Pennylegion had practically no formal education but was a mathematical genius at mentally figuring complicated betting odds.

"And last, but certainly not least," Chief Zulp regained the wandering interest of his audience, "Mayor Phinneas Trutt."

Zulp nodded at his two deputies who had stood beside him through the entire explanation. They put their briefcases on the bench and went down the stairs toward the Mayor's desk at the top of the dais. While they wormed their way through the crowd, Zulp began his summation.

"I know everyone will do his duty. My men have been instructed to be alert at all times. And never leave your side. Within reason. There will be times. Of course. Not really never leave. Everything can be worked out."

He looked over his shoulder. In the middle of the gallery sat two grey-uniformed crossing guards. Zulp stared at them, perplexed. Then he remembered.

"What are you doing *there?*"

The two guards looked at each other.

"You're supposed to be up *here.*"

"But you never called . . ."

"Come, come." Zulp turned back and smiled toward the civil servants. "Henry. Henry Plain. Your guard approaches."

The two pensioners, grumbling under their breath, walked slowly and carefully down the steps to the inner circle.

"One more thing," Zulp said.

Tretheway felt the platform start to sway. It had never been stable, but now both he and Jake detected a slight, but definite, back and forth motion.

"We should be thinking ahead."

The temperature in the room was ninety-eight degrees. There was no movement of air and the humidity was as high as it could be without raining. Cries from the marketplace now sounded irritable. The odour of perspiration displaced the sweet smells that had earlier permeated the air. Several species of flies buzzed noisily.

"Dominion Day. A holiday. July one. Maybe nothing'll happen. Should be on our toes. No cause for alarm. The Master Plan . . ."

A distant rumble of thunder promised relief. Outside the sky darkened, an erratic, welcome breeze swirled around City Hall and the thunder drew nearer and became louder with appropriate, spectacular flashes of lightning. The rain fell, large single drops at first, mixed with hail, and then a torrent which eased to a steady downpour and eventually turned into a warm, gentle drizzle. The small storm had moved quickly through its stages—perhaps no more than ten minutes from warning thunder clap to soft rain. During this time the platform collapsed.

No one was hurt or greatly alarmed. In an extremely slow motion performance, the unique Fort York Council chamber platform snapped some final, inner, key support, which, in turn, ruptured other wires, struts and fasteners and, like a giant cardboard box with no ends, simply folded on itself.

It took the full ten minutes to achieve this. No desks, paper, phones, people—sitting or standing—or anything fell off or were harmed. Gertrude Valentini reached for, but didn't need, her smelling salts. There was little noise and some dust.

When the storm and collapse ended, the Aldermen, Controllers, Police and Mayor were only inches from the floor. They were close to the eye level of the incredulous group of civil servants. In the dream-like silence that followed the miraculous three-tiered descent, Mayor Trutt was the first to react. He tapped his gavel politely. "Lunch."

THE REMAINDER OF JUNE

The funeral went well, as funerals go. Mayor Trutt, Controller Pennylegion, a church elder and a representative from the church (one religious rung higher than Father Cosentino) said the proper words over the well-loved man of God. Although the weather was an improvement over the cloying atmosphere of the Council chamber, the air was still uncomfortably heavy at the graveside. A melancholy, soaking drizzle accompanied the churchman's final eulogy.

After the service, the crowd milled about by threes. Whenever a politician wished to speak to a colleague, it meant a group of six. When three conversed, it meant nine, and so on. The Master Plan was proving unwieldy. But it was working. The reminder of the open grave caused both parties to be over-zealous. If the policemen guarded a little too closely, the politicians didn't object.

"The novelty'll wear off," Tretheway said. "For sure after Dominion Day."

"Do you think something'll happen then?" Jake said.

"It's possible."

"You really think so?" Mac asked.

"Let's put it this way," Tretheway said. "If the crazy bastard kills again, Dominion Day is the most logical time. In his mind, I mean."

"Why?" Mac asked. "And why do you assume he's crazy?"

"It's the next big holiday. There'll be plenty of activity. Good cover. Parades. Parties. And I said, logical. After all, the killer doesn't show that much imagination. Valentine's, St. Patrick's, Victoria Day. What could be more logical than Dominion Day?" Tretheway paused for a moment. "And all murderers are crazy."

"Oh, c'mon, Tretheway," Mac said. "Not that old saw."

"That's right. They can be intelligent after a fashion. High IQ. Appear rational to everyone. But somewhere, somewhere inside their skulls, be it genius or idiot, there's a loose screw. A crossed wire."

33

"There were some, I'm sure, that were completely rational," Mac said. "Some that had a just cause. Perhaps an ideal."

"In their own mind, certainly. But not in the eyes of the law. There's no way you can condone murder."

"What's war then?"

"What the hell's that got to do with it?"

"Just a minute, Boss," Jake interrupted, noticing Tretheway's reddening neck. "You said *if* he kills again. There's some doubt?"

"Yes!" Tretheway shouted. Then more quietly. "Yes."

"How come?"

"I told you before, the Firecracker Day thing didn't sit right."

"Oh?" Mac said.

"At least, I told Jake. Nothing really to go on, Mac. I just don't think it went as planned. By the way, how are your hands?"

"Sore." Mac looked down at his hands and clenched them experimentally. "Doc Nooner says they'll be all right in a couple of weeks."

"That's good."

"Then you're just guessing about Dominion Day," Mac persisted.

"You're absolutely right," Tretheway answered. "I could be full of hot air. I've been wrong before. Eh, Jake?"

"Yes, Sir."

"When?" Tretheway asked.

"Eh?"

"When was I wrong?"

"I don't know. You said it."

"So it's Dominion Day then," Mac asked.

"I think so," Tretheway said.

"But you don't have to worry, Mac," Jake said. "We'll look after you."

"I've been thinking about that, Mac." Tretheway felt in his pocket for a cigar; then remembered he was in uniform. "You'd better move out to the house."

"What for?"

"Just 'till after the holiday. It'll be safer."

"I just can't move in on Addie," Mac protested.

"Either that, or one of us'll have to stay with you. In your apartment."

"I don't know."

"That's settled then." Tretheway looked at Jake. "We'll drive by your place now. You can pick up whatever you need for the next few days."

"Like your cheque book," Jake said.

"What?" Mac asked.

Jake smiled. "For the euchre games."

Tension grew steadily for the next ten days until you could feel it in the air, like fog or drizzle. Everyone followed the Master Plan to the letter. There wasn't one politician left to his own means of protection (not counting Controller Pennylegion). Tretheway, or Jake, or both, kept an eye on MacCulla just about twenty-four hours a day.

Mac moved in as Tretheway suggested. For the first few days, there was almost a party atmosphere, but as Dominion Day approached, there was little anyone could do to change the nervous, expectant mood of the house.

On Saturday evening, the usual card game took place, but with a forced gaiety and banter. There was a second table made up of two young, off-duty policemen, a dour philosophy major and a visiting cheerleader from Toronto U. In the kitchen, two former students (now in RFYLI uniforms) and their dates popped corn. The radio played selections from "Your Hit Parade". Everyone was louder than usual, but Tretheway had the feeling that the house had seen happier times.

Sunday, the last day of the month, began as a day as rare as a day in June. Cottonball clouds scudded across a brazen-blue sky pushed by a refreshing west wind that rustled the leaves of maples and oaks and blew the dust from evergreens. The humidity was low, the temperature was seventy-five and, if the Master Plan could be forgotten for a moment, the day sparkled ahead.

Tretheway, Jake and Fred walked the trails of Coote's Paradise every Sunday afternoon, rain, snow or shine. Fred was a black female Labrador borrowed from a neighbour by Tretheway for these walks. She had been mistakenly named Fred by the neighbour's young son when she was a puppy. The parents couldn't think of any way to change the dog's name to something more suitable, like Frieda or Mary, without hurting the boy's feelings, so Fred it remained. This didn't bother Tretheway since he considered all dogs male anyway and cats female. Today, O. Pitts and MacCulla rounded out the group.

"You know, Boss," Jake said, "we could have a dog of our own."

"You should," Mac said.

"Why?" Tretheway didn't pause in his stride. They were walking in a loose group through the open University property that bordered Coote's Paradise. "Give me one bloody good reason."

"Companionship, loyalty, protection," Jake suggested.

"Always a friendly greeting when you get home," MacCulla aided the cause. "Fun and enjoyment. Chase a ball or stick."

"St. Francis said . . ." O. Pitts began.

"I have enough companions," Tretheway interrupted. "Loyalty I get from the traffic division. I don't need protection. Everybody is reasonably friendly to me when I come home. I have fun and enjoyment playing cards and drinking beer. And, up until today, I haven't thought about chasing a stick or ball."

They slid automatically into single file behind Tretheway at the start of the first trail, helpfully marked "Caleb's Walk" by the Royal Botanical Garden Society.

Tretheway wore an old pair of shiny, navy blue uniform pants and a very large, handsome sweatshirt. He had several of these sweatshirts—some presented to him, some ordered specially by Tretheway himself—in various colours, each with a different crest or motif on the front. This particular one was grey with a small official crest and the words "BUFFALO POLICE GAMES, 1928" emblazoned across the chest. Tretheway crashed aggressively through overhanging trees and stagnant puddles while carefully side-stepping wild flowers and skunk cabbage. Jake followed nervously, arms outstretched to protect himself against the constant backlash of branches from Tretheway's passage. MacCulla strolled, as though in downtown Fort York, in his three-piece business suit. His only concession to nature was a pair of rubbers over his polished brogues. And finally, O. Pitts, very tall, very thin, bobbed up and down and glided over the path in a manner he considered suitably dignified for a potential Baptist minister.

The trail widened and the file regrouped as a disorderly bunch again. They spent the rest of the afternoon enjoying the woods. Mac pointed out various species of trees and bushes, demonstrating unexpected knowledge, and gave an impromptu discourse on the properties of local mushrooms. Jake talked knowingly about Baltimore orioles, tanagers, wild canaries and, at one point, actually spotted, through the overhead lacework of branches, a peregrine falcon high in the sky, slowly circling, soaring gracefully, waiting for a blue jay or water fowl to attract its attention. And Tretheway, to no one's surprise, identified over fifty flowers, ferns, and vines flourishing in the ravine. His success with flowers, including transplanted wild ones, was evidenced every year by the changing display of colour in his own garden. O. Pitts said he saw a deer but nobody believed him.

At different times, they made high, whistling noises with broad leaves on their tongues, chewed on long blades of grass, sniffed the heady, pungent odour that comes from a crumpled sassafrass leaf and threw sticks for the dog, which Fred chased tirelessly even into the marshy waters of Coote's Paradise. The small group made an easy full circle to the end of Princess Point. They walked up the grooved toboggan slides, over the lush green playing fields, back to the residential section and eventually, the Tretheway house. The day was still fresh for late afternoon. They prolonged their pleasure by sitting on the back porch overlooking part of the ravine. Even Fred stayed.

"Isn't tomorrow Dominion Day?" O. Pitts asked. No one answered. "I think it is. Isn't tomorrow the first? Shouldn't Fred go home?"

For over two hours nobody had thought of murder.

JULY

That night, only Controller MacCulla got a good night's sleep. Tretheway commented on this later, at about three in the morning. Everyone had gone to bed around midnight, the official start of Dominion Day, except Tretheway and Jake. They stayed up to check locks on doors and windows and make a final outside inspection. Tretheway checked the garage while Jake walked around the house.

"Everything okay, Jake?"

"Yes, Sir."

"I thought I heard voices."

"That could've been me."

"Who were you talking to?"

"Fred."

"What?"

"She's round the back. Sleeps out next door."

"We're out here in the dark looking for a killer and you're talking to a dog?"

"I'm sorry."

Tretheway shook his head.

The night matched the rarity of the June day. Crickets and the occasional owl could be heard above the nocturnal rustling of the leaves. The moon darted in and around the same clouds that had played tag with the sun during the day. Heavy dew carpeted the grass.

Tretheway crunched along the gravel driveway to the front of the house. Jake followed. Once inside, Tretheway divulged the plans for the night. "We'll take turns watching. I'll go first."

"I can go first," Jake said. "I'm not sleepy."

"No, no. It's about twelve now. I'll wake you at three."

"Right." Jake trundled off to bed.

At three in the morning, the two of them stood, in the glow of the upstairs hall night light, peering into MacCulla's bedroom.

"You'd think," Tretheway said, "he could at least toss and turn a bit."

"He looks awful peaceful." Jake rubbed the sleep from his eye. "Is he okay?"

"Can't you hear him?"

The two listened to the deep, contented snoring of the Controller.

"I'm glad someone can sleep," Jake said.

"A policeman's lot, Jake." Tretheway bent over and picked up three empty beer bottles. "Keep your eyes open."

"Yes, Sir."

"See you at six." Tretheway went to his quarters.

From six to eight, they both alternately dozed and watched over the slumbering Controller. At eight-thirty, Mac awoke, bright and wide-eyed, eager to face the social activities and events of the holiday.

"Let's go, men," he beamed. "Lots to do today."

They breakfasted well, especially MacCulla. Thick porridge cooked by Addie winter and summer, coddled eggs with chives and mushrooms, back bacon and sausages, racks of toast and soft butter or marmalade and strong tea made up the usual menu. Wartime food rationing was in the future.

They discussed procedure in the driveway while they stood beside Jake's car. Tretheway and Jake were in clean dress uniforms; MacCulla sported a natty black pinstripe suit with matching vest.

"Dammit, Jake," Tretheway said, "you should've brought the cruiser home."

"I never thought."

"Why can't I sit in the back?" MacCulla asked.

"Too exposed." Tretheway wrenched open the rumble seat of the '33 Pontiac. "Help me up."

They guided Tretheway up the rear fender steps as well as they could. He stepped into the well, stood poised for a moment on the springy cushion of the seat, then slid helplessly over the worn leather into the small aperture until his girth was wedged against the front and back. His feet almost reached the floor.

"Okay, Boss?"

"Take the back streets."

Jake and Mac climbed into the front seat of the convertible and unbuttoned the rear window. All they could see was Tretheway's middle.

"Comfortable?" Mac asked.

"Get going."

Jake managed to bypass the main parade route by taking the back streets but he couldn't avoid some early spectators. They stared and the bolder ones shouted unkind remarks at the red-faced Inspector jammed halfway into the rumble seat.

At the police garage, Jake discovered that on the bumpy ride from the west end to downtown, Tretheway had become wedged even more firmly into the opening. It was only with the aid of two muscular mechanics that Tretheway regained his freedom. They squatted, one on each rear fender, and hooked their forearms under Tretheway's armpits.

"Sir, this might hurt a little."

"Pull!"

The mechanics pushed themselves slowly upright with the strong muscles of their legs. Tretheway, inhaling drastically, groaned as he slid gradually, rather than popped as everyone expected, out from under the skin of the Pontiac like some bothersome sliver.

"Jake." Tretheway straightened his uniform. "I don't want this to happen again."

"Yes, Sir."

On the way over to City Hall, Tretheway sat in his regular police car seat beside Jake. MacCulla sat in the back.

In observance of the 73rd milestone in Canada's Confederation, picnics were popular, the Dominion Handicap was run at the Fort York Jockey Club, and golf courses were open, but the main event was a parade. It was military in character.

The Royal Fort York Light Infantry Bugle Band, the RFYLI Brass Band, the RFY Artillary Band, the HMCS (stationary) Drum Corp., the STELFY Pipe Band, an Air Force Trumpet Band, various Boy Scout and Sea Cadet Bands and the RFY Ladies' Auxiliary Fifes livened the procession with the overlapping cacophony that makes up a parade.

Jake parked the cruiser beside a hydrant and the three of them walked the short distance to the City Hall. All the politicians insisted on taking the salute. This meant a crowded reviewing stand. Originally, their bodyguards were to be with them, but when it was discovered that the crew who had designed and built the temporary stand over the steep City Hall concrete steps was the same crew responsible for the disastrous Council chamber platform, the police were stationed instead in a protective ring around the structure.

The parade lasted almost two hours. There were two high spots for City Council—at least for MacCulla and Bartholomew Gum. Both their Scout troops were in the parade. Gum's came first; the 42nd Westdale Scout Troop with the older boys marching smartly in unison, Scout hats all at the same rakish angle, the younger ones out of step, trying not to smile at their leader on the podium. It was much the same in Mac's 2nd Fort York Sea Scout Troop, right behind Gum's. The first two pairs marched precisely, older boys again, chins in, chest out, bell-bottoms snapping in the breeze, white lanyards made whiter by the background of navy blue turtle-necks, while the younger Scouts who followed tried unsuccessfully to imitate them.

"Look at those two," Tretheway said, staring up at the reviewing stand.

Jake swiveled his head to watch both Mac and Gum, hands over hearts, eyes sparkling, their puffed pride for a moment overshadowing their rivalry.

"Like mother ducks," Jake said.

"Or peacocks," Tretheway said.

Near the end of the parade, even F. McKnight Wakeley was tired of saluting the endless line of colour parties. The police remained vigilant throughout and the politicians, huddled together on the high stand, were apprehensive at first, but gained confidence with each passing platoon when nothing happened. And nothing did.

After a quick lunch of cold coffee and sandwiches inside the hall, the complete entourage boarded a large bus (policemen standing) and, bracketed by two lorries filled with unarmed militia, drove to the Fort York Civic Stadium for a martial demonstration of calisthenics, close-order drill, mock battles (with eye-stinging smoke screen), marching songs, motorcycle stunts and Highland dancing. After three hours of such entertainment all the bands that were in the parade joined en masse in a deafening, but by this time blessed, finale. The bus then took the company to the Fort York Armory, where a stand-up cocktail hour that stretched into more like two, preceded a stand-up buffet.

The cavernous, high-ceilinged interior of the armory echoed with the conversation of the politicians and their invited guests, a smattering of civil servants, some federal and provincial MPs, Fort York's leading businessmen, newsmen, and, of course, the ubiquitous policemen—hats under their arms and their hands free of drinks. On the balcony that circled three sides of the enclosure, the soldiers from the two lorries stood, evenly spaced, in the at-ease position. The RFYLI Brass Band played Sousa marches in three-quarter time, but few people danced.

Conversation swelled with the cocktails, dropped slightly during the meal and speeches, picked up again with the after-dinner liqueurs and built steadily through the evening with the general opening of the bars and the kegs of draught beer. A few more couples danced, but most just visited. None of the politicians left. However, some stood out more than others.

Henry Plain and his civil servants encircled Alderman Emmett O'Dell as he stood, like Gulliver in Lilliput Land, drinking Irish whiskey and telling off-colour stories of the old sod.

His colleague, F. McKnight Wakely, was doing sit-ups in the officers' washroom.

Old Henry Ammerman told Bartholomew Gum a story that he had told him before, but Gum didn't remember it anyway.

Mayor Trutt reminisced with a group of grey-haired former smoke eaters.

Controller Pennylegion was surrounded, as usual, by swarthy, dark-suited, shifty-eyed companions while, in contrast, MacCulla praised his senior patrol of fair, clean-cut Sea Scouts (soft drinks in their hands) for their part in the parade.

Gertrude Valentini politely refused drinks while abstemious Ingird Tommerup became louder and more physical with each glass of what she thought was ice water given her by a gold-digging suitor.

Alderman Taz and Morgan Morgan argued good naturedly while they got drinks for each other.

And the rest talked on, outwardly oblivious to the possibility of another killing.

The activities of the evening slowed in direct ratio to the hands of the clock. At 11:30 there was a steady murmur of conversation, at 11:45 low whispers and at ten to twelve, relative silence. Politicians looked over their shoulders at other politicians. Policemen strained their eyes searching for something out of place.

Suddenly a waiter fell with a large metal tray of glasses. Gertrude Valentini fainted. The quick, general intake of breath sounded like a giant vacuum cleaner. It took a few long seconds, but when everybody realized what had caused the commotion, relief flooded the armory like laughing gas. The embarrassed laughter and smiles of released tension took up the rest of the time until midnight.

When the hands of the clock passed twelve, there was a roar of resumed chatter. As on New Year's Eve, backslapping and handshakes were the order of the day. Everyone smiled and recharged their glasses—except Tretheway. He wore a puzzled frown and shook his head.

"Can't figure that one out," Tretheway said to Jake.

"Can't guess them all, Boss."

"Something must've happened."

"Eh?"

"To change his mind. His plan."

"Maybe there won't be any more," Jake offered.

"Maybe," Tretheway said. "Let's hope."

A roll of drums from the brass band demanded the attention of the crowd. Chief Zulp made an announcement from the bandstand that reinforced Jake's belief.

"The Master Plan is no longer in effect. It has proven its worth. Good plan. Achieved its objective." He paused, swaying back and forth on the balls of his feet as though he had forgotten the objective. "Protection. Protection of our civic leaders. Of course you'll still be watched. Watched over. Fear not. We'll be there. The Master Plan will be reinvoked the weekend before the next holiday. Which is . . ."

Zulp stared at the crowd. The bandmaster whispered in his ear.

"Civic Holiday," Zulp continued. "August five. It's just a precaution. There will be no more trouble. Speaking as a professional I say the fiend has moved on. To somewhere the police aren't quite as clever."

"Like Toronto!" a Fort York newsman shouted from the floor.

Other good-natured shouts and hollers came from the flushed gathering. Chief Zulp tried to regain their attention but failed and ended up waving to the crowd as he went down the steps of the bandstand.

The party didn't last much longer. After the impetus of relief had burned out, people tired quickly. Tretheway, Jake and MacCulla were home by one-thirty, even having taken the time to pick up Jake's car at Central. This time, MacCulla sat in the rumble seat. He had decided to stay over one more night for convenience sake and return to his apartment the next day. Mac went straight to bed but Tretheway and Jake stayed up for a few minutes, although they were both tired. Tretheway checked the calendar over the sink while he popped a beer.

"August 5, Monday. Civic Holiday." He poured some beer into a glass for Jake.

"Thanks." Jake accepted the glass. "You think something'll happen then?"

"I don't know. I thought something'd happen today."

"But the Master Plan protected us."

"Scared the fiend away."

Jake drained his glass. "I'm beat. Have to go to bed."

"G'night, Jake."

"G'night, Boss."

Jake heard the pop of another beer as he went up the stairs.

The Master Plan wasn't abandoned but it was watered down drastically. Zulp had an obscure but not unrealistic theory that the Cosentino killing was the climax of some mysterious plot, and that therefore nothing else would happen. Politicians were still kept under surveillance during working hours and their homes were checked regularly through the night. But the all-night, sleep-over vigil was discontinued as unnecessary and impractical as a long range plan. Gradually, the FYPD returned to normal police business. And the city returned to normal summertime routine—for wartime.

The factories turned out endless materials for war, which were shipped overland to an eastern port and then convoyed overseas where the people of Britain were beginning their finest hour. Local high schools stayed open during the summer months for the Commonwealth Air Training scheme. The Armory and HMCS Fort York (stationary) did their bit in producing army privates and able seamen. And the University, as well as graduating theologians and arts students, turned out officers and gentlemen with its ROTC course.

At Monday breakfast, July 15, Tretheway and Jake sat in their usual places around the kitchen table. In the large, but somehow intimate room, bacon sizzled, freshly-cut flowers blazed from the table's centre, and the distant doorslams of awakening students punctuated Addie's tuneful humming. Today, instead of morning sunshine, rain was falling. It drummed cosily on the striped canvas awning over the back porch.

"Oh, dear." Addie looked out the window.

"What's the matter?" Jake asked.

"Look at that."

Tretheway and Jake pushed their chairs back and went to the window. They tried to follow Addie's gaze. Tretheway looked easily over her head while Jake stooped slightly and peered through the triangle made by his Boss's arm and side.

Outside, the thick well-kept grass glistened with moisture. Two maples, a mature black walnut, several clumps of white birch, a young oak and an apple tree (fruit half formed and reddening) grew informally about the yard. At the bottom of the garden, healthy evergreens were background for snapdragons, spiky hollyhocks, iris, tall, electric-blue delphiniums, summer phlox and bunches of hardy gold and yellow marigolds. Small white and blue alysum bordered the flower beds. In the rain, all the colours of the garden were tastefully muted.

"What is it?" Tretheway said. "I don't see anything."

"It's raining," Addie said.

"Raining." Tretheway repeated. He looked at Jake.

"Addie, it's summer," Jake said. "It's bound to rain. What's wrong with that?"

"But not today."

"Why not?" Tretheway asked, this time slightly impatient.

"Don't you remember the rhyme we learned at school? For July 15?"

They both shook their heads.

"Oh, you wouldn't, Jake. It's English." Addie looked at Tretheway. "But you should remember."

"Addie. Where's my breakfast?"

She turned from the window and recited, in a classroom, sing-song rhythm:

"St. Swithin's Day, if thou dost rain,
For forty days it will remain;
St. Swithin's Day if thou art fair,
For . . ."

"Jezuz!" Tretheway bolted from the kitchen, almost taking the swinging door with him.

"Albert!" Addie glared after her brother.

Jake steadied the kitchen door while he and Addie followed the Inspector. They found him in the front hall shouting into the phone.

"Swithin's! St. Swithin's! S-W-I, never mind. Where's the Chief?"

"What is it, Boss?"

Tretheway held up his huge hand, palm facing Jake. He barked more orders into the mouthpiece.

"Get every available man down there on the phones. Find out where the Council members are. You must have a list. Tell them to lock themselves in somewhere. Eh?" Tretheway listened for a moment. "I don't know. In the bathroom. Or closet. Or in their cars. Then send someone out to watch them. Every one of them." He listened again. "Cruisers. Their own cars. Bikes. Street cars. I don't care how. Use your head. I'll take full responsibility. And hurry, dammit!" He covered the mouthpiece. "Jake. Jump in your car and check on Ammerman and Bartholomew Gum."

"Right." Jake ran out the front door without questions.

Tretheway uncovered the phone. "We'll look after our ward. Ward three. I'll be here if the Chief calls."

Tretheway slipped the receiver back onto the phone. Several boarders were standing at the bottom of the stairs, attracted by the smell of breakfast and the loud excitable pitch of Tretheway's voice.

"Everything's all right," Tretheway assured them. "I just want to borrow Addie for a few minutes." He motioned to his sister. "Would you come with me, Addie, please?" Tretheway went down the hall into the parlour.

"Oh, dear. Could you look after yourselves?" Addie said to the curious onlookers. "There's porridge on the stove. And tea's brewing." She followed Tretheway.

"Now, Addie. There's nothing to worry about. Just sit here." He indicated the red plush chesterfield. "And tell me all you remember about St. Swithin's Day. I know you're up on these things." Tretheway lowered himself onto the deep, cushiony foot stool in front of his superchair.

"Well," Addie began, "there isn't much to tell. He was an English saint. Ninth century. Saint's Day July 15. He's called the Rain Saint."

"Rain Saint?"

"Yes. That's what the rhyme's all about. He was a very humble man and when he died, he wanted to be buried outside his Cathedral, under the eaves, so that the rain would fall on his grave and the feet of passersby would tread upon it. Isn't that nice?"

"Go on, Addie."

"Well, after he died and was buried there, this Bishop decided to have his body moved inside the cathedral, as it happened, on the 15th of July. Just before the men were to dig him up, it started to rain. For forty days it rained. So the Bishop had to give up his plan. That's why, now, if it rains on St. Swithin's Day, 'For forty days it will remain'." Addie smiled. "Sort of a religious Groundhog Day. Don't you remember?"

"Vaguely. Was there anything else?"

The front door burst open and Jake came in with Alderman Ammerman in tow. They stopped at the parlour entrance.

"That was fast," Tretheway said. "Morning, Harold. Come on in."

"Good morning, Tretheway. Addie." Ammerman stayed in the hall and dripped on the carpet.

Addie jumped up. "Harold, let me take your coat. You're wet. You'll catch your death."

"Nonsense. Never felt better in my life."

Addie shook the rain from Ammerman's coat and carried it to the hall. "Go into the parlour and sit down. What are you doing walking in the rain, anyway?" She hung the coat on one of the large brass hooks jutting out from the wood-framed hall mirror.

"Morning constitutional, Addie. Haven't missed a day in over forty years." Ammerman looked at Jake. "Until this morning. What's going on?"

"Just a precaution, Harold." Tretheway waited for Addie to come in, and then closed the sliding doors to the parlour. He turned to Jake. "Where's Gum?"

"On a hike."

"How do you know?"

"I just caught Alderman Ammerman coming down his front walk. He told me that Bartholomew Gum was up at Mount Nemo. The Scout Camp."

"Where's Nemo, exactly?"

"About ten miles north of Wellington Square."

"When did he go?"

"Friday night. According to the Alderman, it's a weekend thing. You know, hiking, passing badges, sleep in tents, start a fire with one match. They'll be home tonight. Incidentally, MacCulla's there too. With his Scouts."

"Good. Two less to worry about. Now . . ."

"Precautions against what?" Ammerman interrupted.

"Sorry, Harold," Tretheway said. "Today's St. Swithin's Day."

"Why wasn't I told?"

"There was no need for anyone to be told."

"Is there a parade?"

"No, Harold. No. It's just an English Saint's Day. July 15. Like St. George or St. Patrick's Day. Only St. Swithin wasn't as well known."

"Then what's all the fuss?"

For the first time, doubt crept into Tretheway's mind. But he spoke with confidence.

"You know what's been happening around here on holidays. Remember Father Cosentino?"

"Well, yes." Ammerman looked resigned. "I suppose you have your duty."

"Albert," Addie said quietly.

"Hm?"

"There was one other thing. About St. Swithin."

"What was that?"

"Probably not important."

"Addie! Just tell me."

"Well." Addie wriggled herself into a more comfortable position on the chesterfield. "Well," she repeated, "Swithin was a monk. King Egbert of Wessex was having a terrible time defending England against the Danes. They were robbing and slaying a lot across the Channel. The king called all the monks together to help. To slay back. Now, they all did, but Swithin did a better job than the others. So he was awarded . . ."

"Hold it Addie." They all waited while Tretheway lit a cigar. "Just go back a bit."

"To where?"

"Who was Swithin fighting?"

"The Danes. From Denmark."

Tretheway puffed vigorously on his cigar. "Harold, are there any Danish people on the Council?"

"Nope," Ammerman said.

"Wait a minute," Jake interrupted. "Isn't Miss Tommerup Danish?"

"What ward is she from?"

"You're damn right she is. Ingird Tommerup," Tretheway said. "Her father's the President of STELFY."

"Right," Jake said. "Danish as blue cheese."

Tretheway pointed his cigar at Jake. "Get on the phone. See where she lives."

"Right." Jake left the parlour.

"Albert," Addie said. "Surely you don't think . . ."

"Addie, I don't know."

"You know she could be Danish," Ammerman said.

For the next few minutes, Addie sat frowning, Alderman Ammerman looked as though he was trying to remember something and Tretheway puffed on his cigar, oblivious to the ashes falling onto his stomach. Jake came back from the hall phone.

"She's got an apartment in the city. In her ward. But she's not there. I talked to the boys downtown. They phoned her place earlier. Her housekeeper says she's at her summer place for the weekend. In Wellington Square. But she doesn't know the address. It's sort of a retreat. And there's no phone."

"Damn!" Tretheway sat up. Addie ignored the ashes falling to the floor.

"If I might interject for a moment," Ammerman said.

"What is it, Harold?"

"Miss Tommerup's summer place. I know where it is."

"Eh?"

"I remember it quite plainly now. She had a summer party for the Council. Lovely little spot. Quite picturesque. There's a creek . . ."

"Could you take us there?" Tretheway asked.

"Now?" Ammerman frowned. "I think so. Yes."

"I told the boys to call the local police out there," Jake said.

"Red Rounders?" Tretheway asked.

Jake nodded.

Wellington Square was a sleepy village on the North Shore across from Fort York. It had grown to its present situation from a grant of 3500 acres, given to an Iroquois Indian Chief (Thay-endanegea) for his loyalty to the Crown during the American Revolution.

Wellington Square had, among other things, a tree-shaded main street, desirable summer homes, a magnificent sandy beach, two hardware stores, a museum full of arrowheads, and three po-licemen. Two of the policemen were part-time—Saturday night and special occasions.

The only full-time officer was Chief Leonard 'Red' Rounders, a big, outgoing, bucktoothed, thirty-year-old native raised on a local farm. He was well liked by the merchants and did a passable job in the quiet hamlet.

In what could have been his moment of glory, Chief Rounders shot the siren from the fender of the Wellington Square's 1936 Nash police cruiser while in pursuit of a bank robbery getaway car. To be fair, the niggardly village council discouraged revolver practice and actually charged seven cents for each bullet fired by a law officer. The bank robbers were eventually stopped by a road block set up by the Fort York police. Unfortunately, *The FY Expositor* printed the episode of the siren shooting, which was picked up by the wire services across the country. Chief Red Rounders had no love for Fort York, the *Expositor* or the FYPD.

"I hope we get there first," Tretheway said.

"I'll warm the car up." As Jake went out the front door he heard the Inspector ask Ammerman if he knew how to drive. He thought about the seating arrangements with the Alderman at the wheel and sighed. "At least the rain's off," he said, looking at the sky.

Ammerman weaved the car backwards out of the driveway under Jake's nervous guidance from the rumble seat. Tretheway stared straight ahead from the passenger seat. The phone rang inside the house.

"Just a minute," Addie shouted from the verandah. "It might be for you." She disappeared.

The trio stayed in the car. Jake leaned through the small aperture in the back curtain, pushing his arm between the two in the front seat to point out the unfamiliar instruments to the seventy-three-year-old Alderman.

Addie came back. "It's Chief Zulp, Albert. He wants to speak to you. And he doesn't sound very friendly."

Tretheway turned as far as he could toward her. "Tell him we've gone," he shouted. "Let's go, Harold."

The car jerked away over the centre line, then back again, scuffing the curb. Addie waited and watched until the car turned the last corner, bumped over another curb and went out of sight. She went back into the house and picked up the phone.

"I'm sorry, Chief Zulp, but Albert's gone to work."

It took Ammerman a full hour to find the street. At first they had driven, sure of their geography, down the big hill that skirts Coote's Paradise to the city limits, then along Highway #2 passing miles of farmland, LaSalle Park, the venerable Wellington Square Golf and Country Club and some summer homes, until they reached Beach Boulevard. Here, at Ammerman's insistence, they turned right (the wrong way) and drove for a mile along the strip that separates Fort York Harbour from Lake Ontario. Then, at Tretheway's insistence, Ammerman made an illegal U-turn and drove back into the village. After several other false starts, they found themselves on what Ammerman said was Ingird Tommerup's street.

"I'm positive this is it," Ammerman said.

"Do you see the house?" Tretheway asked.

The Alderman strained his weak eyes through the flat, upright glass of the windshield. There were no people about. And the grey skies and lowering clouds promised more rain.

"There!" Ammerman shouted. "Where that car is."

The car was a 1936 Nash sedan with a new siren.

"Damn!" Tretheway glared at Ammerman. "Too many wrong turns."

"I knew I could find it." Ammerman turned sharply up the driveway and braked as hard as he could, but still bumped into the police car with enough force to throw his upper body onto the horn.

"Jezuz!" Tretheway said.

Jake jumped out and closed the rumble seat.

"Those brakes don't feel right, Jake," Ammerman said, climbing out of the driver's seat. The two watched the Pontiac dip noticeably as Tretheway, grunting, lifted himself by the sturdy window post onto the running board and dropped to the ground.

They stood quietly. There was little wind and no sound of birds. The silence was broken by a lonesome whistle from a distant impatient lake freighter and the first drops of light rain falling on the canvas roof of the car.

"That's odd," Tretheway said.

"Rounders must've heard us." Jake looked at Ammerman.

"Check the back, Jake," Tretheway ordered. "I'll try the front door."

"If I might interject . . ."

"Harold. You stay here."

Tretheway was halfway to the cottage when Jake shouted.

"Here! Around here!"

Tretheway covered the distance with surprising speed. Jake was kneeling beside the prostrate form of Wellington Square's finest—Chief Rounders. He was flat on his back, arms and legs stiffly and symmetrically outstretched to form the five points (counting his head) of a star that resembled an oversized children's party cookie.

"What's the matter with him?" Tretheway asked.

"I don't know," Jake said. "I think he's fainted."

Ammerman hovered nervously behind Jake. Tretheway looked a full suspicious circle for anything out of the ordinary.

"He's coming around," Jake said.

Chief Red Rounders groaned, his eyelids fluttered and opened as his eyeballs dropped into view like two blue oranges in a slot machine. Jake gently patted his cheeks. "Red. Red Rounders. Are you okay?"

The Wellington Square Chief groaned again and said something.

"What'd he say?" Tretheway asked.

Jake helped the Chief to a sitting position. "I can't hear you, Red." Red Rounders slowly raised his freckled hand and pointed behind Tretheway. His mouth worked. "R . . . rain."

As though at a signal, the rain became heavier. The familiar hackles rose on Tretheway's neck as he remembered Addie's innocent remark about the Rain Saint. He turned and stared in the direction of Rounder's accusatory finger. The natural shapes of small trees, bushes, vines and tall weeds obscured the corner of the cottage. Tretheway squinted. He saw something else, something too stiff and foreign, an irregular shape that didn't belong in nature. Tretheway started toward it.

"Hold it, Boss," Jake said. "Maybe we should wait."

Tretheway ignored the warning. He ducked under a pair of apple trees, walked around a large forsythia and pushed his way through the weeds and scraggly bushes toward the cottage. The rain water from the shrubbery dripped freely from his patent leather peak onto his nose. His thirty-two calibre officer's issue revolver remained, as usual, jammed into his leather-lined pocket. He stopped at the corner of the summer cottage where an old-fashioned rain barrel stood under the downspout from the roof.

"Jezuz!" Tretheway said.

It was overflowing, partly because of the wet weather and partly because of Ingird Tommerup.

"Jake. You'd better come here."

Jake appeared, carrying a large, wicked-looking crooked stick instead of his revolver which he had left in his desk. Ammerman and a groggy Red Rounders were right behind him. They crowded around Tretheway and stared in the rain barrel.

"Gawd!" Jake said. Ammerman's jaw moved soundlessly up and down. Red Rounders sat down again on the wet grass. His hat fell off.

The bare, hairy, muscular legs of Ingird Tommerup, knees locked, stuck straight out of the full rain barrel. She wore scruffy yellow bowling shoes. Her thick navy blue bloomers were visible just below the surface of the water.

"Let's get her out of there." Tretheway grabbed a leg. Jake, hesitating only for a moment, grabbed the other. They struggled with her, cold and stiff and slippery from the rain, until finally Ingird lay on the ground, her long flaxen hair, heavy with water, stretched out behind her.

"Is she . . .?" Jake started.

"Yes," Tretheway said. "Hours ago, I'd say." He froze suddenly. "Jake."

"Mm?"

"What's that?" Tretheway pointed to a reddish mark on the fleshy part of Ingird's thigh. Jake forced himself to look closely. The weak daylight picked up an indentation in the skin: a perfectly formed cross about an inch and a half square.

"I don't know," Jake answered. "Looks like an emblem of some sort."

"A cross."

"That's right. A Maltese cross."

"Peculiar." Tretheway straightened up. "We'll just keep this to ourselves. At least, 'till Wan Ho gets here."

Jake agreed.

"And get something to cover her up."

Red Rounders pushed himself to his feet. "There's a tarp in my car." He recovered his hat and shook the rain from it. "I'll get it."

"You'd better look for a phone, Jake," Tretheway said. "Try down the street."

Jake jogged the two hundred yards to the nearest neighbour and phoned in. In the fifteen to twenty minutes it took the Fort York police to arrive—plus all the necessary ancillary groups—Tretheway and Jake searched the cottage and grounds. First, Tretheway took Ammerman inside the cottage out of the rain.

"Make some tea or something," Tretheway said.

"Tea," Ammerman said, neither question nor answer, but a simple repetition. It was the first word he had managed since he had seen the rain barrel.

In the cottage Tretheway found little to enlighten him. It was untidy, but not in disarray. Miss Tommerup's purse lay on the kitchen table full of money, two expensive fur coats hung in the front hall and one of her dresser drawers, which Tretheway quickly shut, held a week's supply of clean navy blue bloomers. He raised his eyebrows at the man's safety razor in the medicine cabinet.

Outside, even with Jake's help (Red Rounders was guarding the body and tarpaulin), Tretheway found no helpful clues. The grass around the rain barrel was thick and springy, hardly ideal material for footprints, and the muddy areas around the puddles had either been avoided or unvisited. By the time the first police arrived, all that Tretheway and Jake had found between them were seven arrowheads.

Sergeant Charlie Wan Ho was in the first car with four other detectives. He made straight for Tretheway.

"Hi, Inspector." He smiled at Jake.

"Hello, Charlie," Tretheway said. Jake smiled back.

"Please don't say it's another murder."

"I'm sorry."

"Damn! Is it Miss Tommerup?"

Tretheway nodded.

In the many years Sergeant Wan Ho had been on the force, he had tried to develop a hard-nosed, indifferent, professional attitude toward death. He blew his nose violently.

"Zulp here yet?" Tretheway asked.

"Not yet," Wan Ho said. "I'm sure he's on his way. Like to catch me up?"

Tretheway brought the Sergeant up to date from Addie's first mention of St. Swithin's Day to the present. Wan Ho stood quietly, nodding occasionally, taking in the information, mentally filing, evaluating and planning. When Tretheway finished (except for the mysterious cross) Wan Ho asked a couple of perceptive questions and then snapped out orders to the waiting detectives. They scattered—one in the cottage, two to search the grounds and the fourth to knock on neighbouring doors.

"Can I see the body now?" Wan Ho asked.

"This way." Tretheway started walking. He looked sideways at Jake. "As a matter of fact, I'd like you to see something else."

Wan Ho's face, never inscrutable, showed a flicker of interest. The three of them squatted around the body. Tretheway lifted the tarpaulin.

"Doc Nooner hasn't been here yet, but I'm sure she drowned. A while ago, too." Wan Ho nodded again while Tretheway went on. "Of course, we'll be interested in his opinion. But just for now, what do you think of that?" Tretheway pointed to the mark just above Miss Tommerup's knee.

Wan Ho leaned forward. "What do I think of what?"

"Right there. That red mark."

"It's just a red mark."

"You've got to get it in the proper light." Tretheway bent closer. "Damn. Can you see anything from your side, Jake?"

Jake leaned closer. "I think it's faded."

"What's faded?" Wan Ho asked.

Tretheway looked again. "I think you're right. It's gone."

"What's gone?" Wan Ho was close to shouting.

"A cross," Tretheway said.

"A what?"

"So help me," Jake said. "A perfect Maltese cross."

Wan Ho looked again. "Well, it's not there now." He stood up. "Are you sure?"

"Yes." Tretheway replaced the tarp. "Jake saw it too."

"That's right," Jake confirmed.

"Now let me get this straight." Wan Ho organized his thoughts. "You saw an impression of a cross. A Maltese cross. Actually indented in the skin of Miss Tommerup."

"As plain as day," Tretheway said.

"Well, what's it mean? A signal? A sign of some sort?" Wan Ho shook his head. "This is real Charlie Chan stuff."

"Chief Zulp'll know what it means," Jake said.

"Maybe we shouldn't mention it," Tretheway said. "For the time being," he added.

"It might be the best thing," Jake agreed.

They looked at Wan Ho.

He shrugged. "I didn't even see it."

That night, as Tretheway lay on his double-mattressed, double-springed bed listening to the wet rustling of the oak leaves outside his bedroom window, he wondered, just before he dropped off, whether it would rain for forty more days.

"All right, Tretheway. I don't want any more surprises."

Tretheway was standing rigidly at attention in front of Chief Zulp's desk. He had been summoned there first thing. It was Monday morning again, seven days after the murder of Ingird Tommerup; seven long, arduous and disappointing days for the FYPD—especially for Zulp.

"Do you know how many people have called me every day? Including the week-end?" Zulp continued.

Tretheway shook his head needlessly. Zulp stretched out the stubby fingers of one hand and jabbed at them with the index finger of the other, enumerating the callers.

"The Mayor. Always the Mayor first. Then the judges that sit with him on the Police Commission. Then that damn *Expositor.* Twice a day. And today, I had my first call from Edgar Tommerup. The deceased's father. President of STELFY. Very important man. Influential."

Tretheway nodded imperceptibly, still at attention.

"He was very angry. To put it mildly. Sore as a bloody bull. Threatened to use the STELFY Security Police to find the killer. His very own homicide squad. Can't do that. Illegal. Took me aback, though. He was so polite at the funeral."

"Sir?"

"Eh?"

"You said something about surprises?"

"I did?"

"When you first called me in." Zulp thought for a moment. "That's right," he said finally. "Surprises. I don't want any more surprises, Tretheway. Like the twenty-fourth of May. Or Father's Day. Or this last one. St. Whatshisname's Day."

"Swithin's."

"Let's get down to business. What's all this scuttlebutt about you? Your predictions. Did you have prior knowledge of these events? A hunch? A lucky guess? As I understand it, you weren't as surprised as me. I suggest you clear this up. From the beginning. Sit down."

Tretheway let his breath out and his chest down. Squatting gingerly, he squeezed between the arms of the office chair. "As you remember, St. Valentine's Day and St. Patrick's Day caught us all by surprise. And they were still just pranks. When April Fool's Day came along, it set a pattern. Once a month, holidays, politicians. But still a prank."

"That's correct."

"It was at this time that I said, more as conversation than anything else, that the next logical holiday for our man to strike was the twenty-fourth of May."

"Why the twenty-fourth?"

"It seemed to fit the pattern. The flamboyance. Fireworks as the method. I made an educated guess. A lucky one."

"What about Father's Day?"

"Also logic. It's the only holiday to speak of. Now don't forget, it was still in the nature of a guessing game. No one had been killed."

"But what about St. Swithin's Day? You're the one that called out half the bloody force. On your own initiative. And too late."

"I know." Tretheway looked worried. "I thought something would happen on Dominion Day. I'd forgotten about St. Swithin's Day until my sister Addie reminded me."

"How did she know?"

"She didn't. There was a rhyme we memorized as kids about St. Swithin's Day. Addie recited it that morning. When I asked her about it, she went into the whole story."

"Spare me that. But why St. Swithin's?" Zulp prompted impatiently. "No one's ever heard of it."

"I'm not sure. Maybe the killer's trying to confuse us. Keep us off balance."

Zulp smacked his fist loudly into the palm of his other hand. "Couldn't agree more!"

"Sir?" Tretheway was always amazed when his superior's train of thought leaped sideways like a rabbit escaping a predator.

"I've been doing some homework," Zulp confided. "Come up with some facts. Startling." He stared at the ceiling. Tretheway waited.

"When's the next one?" Zulp lowered his gaze. "Civic Holiday? Labour Day? Hallowe'en? Will there be another one? And who's the victim? Would you like to guess, Tretheway?"

"Not really, Sir."

"I wish you would, Tretheway."

Tretheway knew an order when he heard one. He cleared his throat. "Well, I'd say if anything does happen, it would be in August."

"Go on," Zulp encouraged.

"And, once again, the logical day would be Civic Holiday. Let's see." Tretheway checked the Stanley Cup wall calendar showing the World Champion New York Rangers. "The first Monday in August. Two weeks today. August five."

"Nonsense!"

"Sir?"

"And who's the victim?"

"That would definitely be a guess. Nobody knows."

"I do."

Tretheway stared at Zulp for a moment. "Sir, if you have any new information . . ."

"I have the same information you have, Tretheway," Zulp interrupted.

"Nothing new?"

Zulp shook his head. "Think, Tretheway. Use the old noodle." Zulp rubbed his hands together. "It won't wear out, you know."

"I'm sorry, Sir. I don't understand."

"Aha!" Zulp jumped up and started pacing excitedly. "Tretheway. Do you know what the twenty-fourth of August is?"

Tretheway checked the calendar again. "It's a Saturday."

"Nothing else?"

"Not that I know of."

"Exactly." Zulp sat down again. He leaned back in his chair, and basked in the warmth of withheld knowledge. But he couldn't contain himself. "The twenty-fourth of August is St. Bartholomew's Day!"

Tretheway tried to look as though he'd just heard something meaningful.

"Do you know who St. Bartholomew is?" Zulp asked.

Tretheway shook his head without changing his expression.

"An apostle," Zulp explained. "Of royal birth. Spent a life of hardship as a missionary. Met a tragic end. An Armenian hung him up on a cross. Head downward and flayed him alive."

"Flayed?"

"Skinned." Zulp rummaged in his desk drawer, ostensibly looking for a toothpick, but really to refresh his memory with the notes he had made at the library while poring over an obscure book entitled *High Days the World Over.* He found both. "St. Bartholomew had a special power over thunderstorms. Also cured people of rare diseases. Like catalepsy." Zulp fenced with a stubborn piece of back bacon wedged between two molars. "But here's the zinger, Tretheway. In the olden days, in some churches, they'd give knives to the congregation to mark St. Bartholomew's Day. Because of the flaying. Matter of fact, he appears with a knife in more than one famous painting." Zulp narrowed his eyes at Tretheway. "Now doesn't that give you any ideas?"

"Ah, not right away."

"Then how about"—Zulp cleared his throat—'St. Bartholomew/Brings the cold dew.' "

Zulp kept staring at Tretheway. Tretheway shook his head.

"Who are the Aldermen in ward three? Your ward." Zulp asked.

"Ah . . . Ammerman and Gum."

"Gum?"

Zulp smiled knowingly. "And what's his first name?"

"Bartholomew."

"Exactly." Zulp rose from his chair. He felt that his next statement was much too important to be made from a sitting position. "On August the twenty-fourth, early in the morning when the dew lies on the grass, the politician Bartholomew Gum will be stabbed to death. Or maybe flayed."

After an awkward pause, Tretheway spoke. "I don't believe it."

"Neither did I at first," Zulp said. "But logic and reason persisted. Discipline in thought, Tretheway."

"There's just one thing, though."

"Hm?"

"Well, to simplify matters, St. Swithin killed Vikings. And on St. Swithin's Day, a Viking was killed. That's Miss Tommerup."

"So?" An edge of suspicion crept into Zulp's voice.

Tretheway attempted to twist into a more comfortable position. The chair twisted with him. "You're saying that on St. Bartholomew's Day, someone called Bartholomew will be killed. With a knife. Now to follow the pattern, shouldn't someone who Bartholomew killed in legend be murdered?"

"What do you mean?"

Tretheway bit his thin lips and plowed on. "St. Swithin killed Vikings. Who did St. Bartholomew kill?"

"I told you what he did, dammit! He did things with lightning. Cured sick people. He had a knife."

"But who did he kill?"

Zulp didn't answer.

"I mean," Tretheway persisted, "he didn't kill anyone called Bartholomew, did he?"

Zulp placed his beefy, clenched fists on his desk blotter and leaned toward Tretheway. His voice was controlled. "If you can't follow a simple, straightforward line of reasoning, it's just as well your duties are confined to the Traffic Department."

Tretheway, realizing the discussion was over, jumped to his feet. The chair came with him.

"I repeat, Tretheway. Your duties are confined to the Traffic Department."

Tretheway pushed the chair off his backside and saluted.

AUGUST

In July, 1669, Sieur de LaSalle set sail from Ville-Marie (Montreal) in search of the Ohio River in order "not to leave to another the honour of finding the way to the Southern Sea and thereby the route to China." Two months later, he entered Fort York Harbour. The expedition anchored off the North Shore across the bay from the future site of Fort York. A small boat ferried a landing party to shore where LaSalle himself jumped out and became the first white man to set foot on the sandy beach.

In 1922, the Fort York Historical Society fastened to a large, immovable, but convenient boulder resting on a bluff above the historic landing a bronze plaque that briefly described the French explorer's feat. The city purchased the surrounding five acres and named it, appropriately, LaSalle Park.

Every Civic Holiday, the City of Fort York threw a mammoth picnic at the park for all city employees, including policemen, firemen and local politicians. Everyone would remember the 1940 Civic Holiday.

"Don't crush the sandwiches, Albert," Addie said.

"Never mind me," Tretheway said, clutching the many cumbersome bundles of food Addie had carefully prepared for the picnic. "Make sure he doesn't drop the beer." He jerked his head back toward Jake, who was struggling and clinking with the day's supply of Molsons.

"Are you all right, Jake?" Addie asked.

Jake smiled stoically. The ice that surrounded the beer he was carrying melted rapidly under the hot sun. It ran out through the small holes in the old dented wash tub, soaked his white shorts and mixed with the perspiration on his thin bony legs. "Just fine, Addie."

Even in his discomfort, Jake admired the way Addie easily carried the cutlery, an umbrella, several books and magazines, her knitting and a heavy blanket, and still managed to look fresh. She wore a flowered summer dress with a matching floppy-brimmed picture hat. Controller MacCulla rounded out their party. He was there partly by choice; partly because the Master Plan had been re-invoked for the Civic Holiday. But as Chief Zulp had confidently announced on the evening before the holiday, "Stay on your toes, men. But don't worry. Tomorrow will only be a rehearsal for St. Bartholomew's Day."

Tretheway's party found an empty table about fifty feet from LaSalle's rock. For the next fifteen minutes, they settled in comfortably for the holiday. Addie cleaned the table and covered it with the heavy blanket. The knives, forks, glasses and paper plates were arranged into four place settings. Jake stored the beer under the table along with Addie's umbrella and reading matter. Addie placed her hat on the table over her knitting while Tretheway threw his navy blue blazer on top of both.

"Be careful, Albert," Addie said.

Tretheway grunted, but folded his coat neatly and placed it on the bench beside him with the colourful, 2nd Life Guards' crest in plain sight. Jake kicked off his wet tennis shoes while MacCulla uncharacteristically loosened his tie and undid the top button of his vest. Addie handed out cold bottled beer to Tretheway and Jake, poured her own in a glass and gave MacCulla his first lemonade of the day. They sat back, finally—Tretheway on one side of the table, Addie, Mac and Jake on the other—to begin the day's enjoyment.

From under their stand of mature red maples, they had a flattering view of Fort York. Two miles across the sail-studded blue water of the harbour, the late morning sun dramatically picked out the white puffballs of train smoke and, at the same time, softened the man-made skyline of steel-making equipment. In back of the industrial area came office buildings and then residences, marching in orderly fashion to the limestone ridge of Fort York Mountain. And sprinkled generously throughout the picture were green, green trees.

"Here comes the *Lady York!*" someone shouted.

The Tretheway party had driven around the bay in an unmarked '39 Mercury police car, partly because they were on police business (guarding MacCulla) and partly because Tretheway disliked water, particularly boat rides. Most of the crowd was expected to arrive on the *S.S. Lady York,* an old but seaworthy ferry that made several return trips every navigable summer's day from a public dock at the foot of Fort York's ward two to LaSalle Park. In minutes, it was at the dock below them.

Tretheway watched as the excited crowd ran toward the starboard side gangway. The ferry listed slightly while people spewed from the *Lady York's* innards. A small crowd of disembarking civil servants remained dockside to watch a calisthenics demonstration put on by a hand-picked group of older Scouts.

"Watch this, everyone," Mac said.

Four of his Sea Scouts started their performance. Even from a distance Tretheway was impressed by the obvious training and discipline of this young group. The Scouts bounced up and down on the balls of their feet, opening and closing their stances while alternately clapping their hands above their heads and slapping their thighs, all in perfect unison. As part of a memorized plan, they would switch to another exercise, increase the tempo, then switch to yet another. They glowed with health. At the end of their last exercise, the Scouts stood stiffly at attention. The sound of polite applause filtered up to the picnic area from the wharf. MacCulla smiled broadly.

During the demonstration, Henry Plain and group had taken the next table. There were twice as many in the City Clerk's party as in the Tretheways'; but they took up the same amount of space. The two parties exchanged waves.

"I wish they hadn't sat there," Tretheway said.

"They're good people, Boss," Jake said.

"They're too damn small."

"Albert! They'll hear you," Addie said.

Tretheway popped a Molson.

The children's races and games started at a medically sensible interval (determined by Dr Nooner) after lunch. For the next while Tretheway and party were entertained from a distance by the thudding of juvenile feet, the blowing of whistles and the presentation of prizes. Cheers rose whenever a winner crossed the finish line or won an event—which was often.

"Good kids," Tretheway said.

"A pleasure to watch," Jake said.

Addie smiled.

"Look at Controller Pennylegion." Tretheway indicated another table, apart from the rest and closer to the road, where the Pennylegion bunch sat.

As usual, Pennylegion himself sat in the centre of his group. Surrounded as he was by hirelings dressed in black and medium grey, Joseph Pennylegion stood out in his immaculate white flannel shirt, white shoes, dark trousers, and wildly designed red and purple tie that matched his hat band and clashed with his hair. Even from four or five tables away, his jewelled stick pin sparkled noticeably. Pennylegion's bunch, with the exception of the two ill-at-ease police guards stationed at either end of the table, was drinking a local red wine. Their black Packard was parked close to them on the grass. A man called Crank, reportedly an expert driver, sat on the running board cleaning his nails.

"What about Pennylegion?" Jake asked Tretheway quietly. Addie and Mac were busy talking to some of the Plain people at the next table. "Is he clean?"

"As far as I know, yes. His past is . . . obscure. Nobody seems to know much about him. You know all the rumours about his trucks. During Prohibition. But, according to Wan Ho, there's no record."

"He sure looks the part."

"I wouldn't bat an eye if Edward G. Robinson sat down with him."

"Or George Raft."

"Certainly not Warner Oland."

"Or William Powell."

The two chuckled. Tretheway stood up and made a spectacle of stretching. "Let's go for a walk."

Jake stood also. "You expecting anything?"

"It won't hurt to move around."

"You think that today, maybe, being a holiday and all that . . ." Jake swallowed. ". . . something might happen?"

"The Chief says not today."

"I know. St. Bartholomew's Day. But what do you think?"

Tretheway moved away from the table. He looked squarely at Jake. "I hope nothing happens. I hope the whole train of events has been a series of ridiculous coincidences. A bunch of practical jokes topped off by an unrelated strangling and a stupid drowning."

Tretheway continued to stare but Jake wouldn't look away.

"Today," Tretheway said finally. "I think something'll happen today." He looked back at the table. "Let's go, Mac."

"Hm?" Mac was pouring his second lemonade.

"C'mon," Jake said to Mac. "We're going for a walk."

"No, thank you. I'll stay here."

"You have to go, Mac," Tretheway said. "The Master Plan. It's time for your ball game anyway."

"We won't be long, Addie." Jake smiled. Addie smiled back. The three of them started off.

"How's the investigation going, anyway?" Mac asked.

"Not too well," Tretheway said.

"Depends which paper you read," Jake added.

The investigation was *not* going too well and it *did* depend on which paper you read. Toronto papers, still smarting from last year's humiliating football season at the hands and feet of the Fort York Taggers, said the case was being "badly botched". "The leader of the investigation," the quote continued, "the old right winger himself, has once again dropped the ball in his own end zone." This was an uncalled for, but true, reference to the finale of Chief Zulp's football career that occurred the last time Toronto beat the FY Taggers on a sunny autumn afternoon in 1927.

The local *Fort York Expositor,* on the other hand, with several impressive but mysterious references to a secret Master Plan, said that the Department, led by Chief Zulp, was zeroing in on the lone religious fanatic, but "at this time, because of security reasons, was unable to release a statement". In between these two views, with perhaps a slight leaning toward the Toronto papers, lay the truth.

Nothing newsworthy had been uncovered. Zulp still backed the Single Perpetrator theory against Dr Nooner's conflicting More-Than-One hypothesis—in Ingird Tommerup's homicide as well as Father Cosentino's. Sergeant Wan Ho had done all he could under the circumstances. Regular criminals had been rounded up, questioned and released. The alibis and whereabouts of all concerned parties had been checked out with no damning conclusions. In a search for possible eyewitnesses, neighbours had been interrogated, leads run to sterile ground, with the result that, as Wan Ho put it in his Charlie Chan voice, "No suspects, therefore, all suspects."

Tretheway led Jake and Mac toward the pavilion. This year, as usual, it had been freshly painted for the holiday. The glossy white walls and columns stood out clearly in the park and contrasted sharply with the bright blue trim and matching shingles. A sturdy, weather-vaned cupola rose from the roof.

They mounted the shallow steps and slid across the concrete floor which was already sprinkled with sand for the evening dance. Tretheway made his way through a crowd of boisterous children to the inside hot dog stand. He held up two thick fingers to the concessionnaire.

"You want anything, Jake?" He looked over his shoulder. "Mac?"

"No thanks," Jake said. Mac shook his head.

They went down the steps on the other side of the pavilion, Tretheway clutching a hot dog in each hand.

"Should we be looking for anything special?" Jake asked. "Or should we be looking at all?"

"What's that mean?" Tretheway asked.

"I thought Zulp said . . ." Jake hesitated.

"That I was to confine myself to traffic duties," Tretheway finished. He ate his first hot dog in three bites.

"Then what should we do?" Jake asked.

"What we always do. Follow orders."

"Oh."

Tretheway finished his second hot dog. "However. A policeman is on twenty-four hour duty. A detective can write a parking ticket. A desk man can deliver a baby. A motorcycle patrolman can stop a bank robbery. And a Traffic Inspector," he smiled at Jake, "or his able assistant, can arrest a murderer."

Jake smiled.

"I hope you know what you're doing," Mac said.

"You just stay close," Tretheway said with an edge to his voice.

The trio skirted two smaller buildings the same colour and architecture as the larger pavilion, except for "Ladies" and "Gentlemen" painted on the white walls. Conversation was pointless as they passed the wading pool, filled with squealing children and surrounded by mothers with worried looks and wet towels. They bypassed two temporary hot dog stands, a busy multiple horseshoe pitch, a pick-up football game, all the while dodging children and adults going to or coming from other activities in the large park.

At the edge of the softball field, behind the right foul line well out of play, stood a ridiculously large, conical pile of newspapers at least forty feet high. The area schoolchildren had spent weeks gathering the paper, house to house, store to store, farm to farm, in a remarkable show of patriotism for the war effort. LaSalle Park had been selected as a convenient depository.

"That's the biggest pile of paper I've ever seen." Jake said. "Those kids deserve a lot of credit."

"It's for a good cause, Jake," Tretheway said.

"Mac." Jake pointed toward home plate. "Isn't that your team warming up?"

They noticed most of the Fort York politicians milling around in front of the backstop screen, kicking the dust, gossiping, exercising lightly; two of them were actually tossing a softball around.

Mac appeared excited. "You're right, Jake," He loped off toward the group.

For the members of the City Council, the high point of the picnic was the baseball game. Each year the Mayor, the Board of Control and all the ward Aldermen faced a handpicked team of civic employees in a five-inning (they'd never finished) half-serious, grudge match. The civic team, having so many departments to choose from, were unfairly superior. They played a lackadaisical game. The politicians, on the other hand, played as competitively and aggressively as they could. In twenty-one consecutive picnic games, the elected officials of Fort York had never won.

"Play ball!" Henry Plain shouted from behind home plate in a voice surprisingly deep for his size. The City Clerk traditionally umpired the ball game because his category was not as clear-cut as say, a Controller or garbageman. "Neither fish nor fowl," as Mayor Trutt humorously put it. Henry wore a chest protector and mask borrowed from a city-sponsored bantam team.

Because of the numerical advantage of the civic employees and the age difference between the two teams, the politicians were allowed to field their whole group of ten. Mayor Trutt, leader in the Council and leader on the field, (his own slogan), pitched to Joseph Pennylegion who affected a loud, talk-it-up style of catching. F. McKnight Wakeley, in his summer drill uniform, played first base, Bartholomew Gum second, Emmett O'Dell shortstop with MacCulla rounding out the infield at third base. He had taken off his tie.

From where Tretheway sat behind the third base line, he could hear Morgan Morgan in left field within conversation distance of Taz in centre field. They both carried hip flasks. Ammerman in right field chatted with Gertrude Valentini, who had been officially designated outfield rover.

"One thing, Jake," Tretheway said. "It makes our job easier."

"Hm?" Jake said.

"The baseball game. Gets them all together. We can keep our eye on Mac. And all the other officers can watch their charges." Tretheway waved his hand across the field of players. "Our city fathers. All together in one bundle. One convenient bunch. Every . . ." He stopped short.

"What's the matter?" Jake asked.

Tretheway stared at the inept group of politicians as though he had just seen them for the first time.

"What is it?" Jake persisted.

"If you were the killer," Tretheway proposed, "and, just for fun, had decided to do away with the whole City Council . . ." He lit a cigar.

"Go on," Jake encouraged.

"You've carried out a few pranks. You've eliminated Father Cosentino. Then Miss Tommerup. Both successfully. Your confidence is growing. Now here's an opportunity where they're all together. In one spot. I mean, this game was no secret. What would you do?"

"Ah . . . I don't know." Jake craned his neck and checked the parking lot, the pavilion and even the distant woodlots. He saw plenty of people but they were all doing what they were supposed to do. "But, all of a sudden, I feel nervous."

"Why?" Tretheway asked.

"Because of what you just said."

"Oh hell, Jake. That's all conjecture. Top of my head. Nothing'll happen right now."

"How can you tell?"

"It's just not his style." Tretheway brushed ashes from his front. "Doesn't fit the pattern. And there's no joke about it. Stop worrying."

"All the same." Jake checked the crowd again.

"For one thing," Tretheway suggested, "how do you know the killer isn't out there right now?"

"Out where?"

"Playing baseball?"

Jake stared Tretheway full in the face. "You mean . . . that . . . you're saying . . ."

"Jake, Jake." Tretheway leaned over and squeezed both Jake's knees together with one hand as a young boy might squeeze the straws in his rival's soda. "I'm not saying anything. Just thinking out loud. Watch the game. And keep your eye on Mac. I'm going for a beer." He stepped off in the direction of their picnic table, puffing smoke. Jake rubbed the feeling back into his knees and turned his attention to the game.

There were no real surprises in the baseball game this year either. It went just about the way everyone expected, even with the new rules. One of them allowed the City Council pitcher six balls instead of the customary four, but Mayor Trutt still managed to load the base on balls twice in the first inning.

By the time the politicians came to bat, the score was 17 to 0 and they had lost one of their players. Ammerman had collided with a friendly English sheep dog in mid-field chasing a fly ball that Lucifer Taz had subsequently caught and dropped. So that when Tretheway arrived back refreshed, he found old Ammerman beside Jake, sitting on the grass.

"What happened?" Tretheway asked.

"Slight collision." Jake nodded at Ammerman. "Just knocked the wind out of our friend."

"It was a good clean check," Ammerman wheezed.

"What's the score?" Tretheway asked.

"Seventeen to nothing," Jake said.

"Hm." Tretheway watched the politicians at bat.

Pennylegion got a hit and held at first base, but Trutt, Wakeley and Bartholomew Gum went down two, three, four. In minutes the City Council was out in the field again.

What Mayor Trutt lacked in pitching ability, he made up in shouts. He shouted at all the infield for being out of position (which they were) every time a run was scored; he shouted at Henry Plain for all his unfavourable calls; and he shouted at Controller Pennylegion every time he dropped a wild pitch. Pennylegion knew baseball, particularly the betting odds, and had an accurate, strong throw. Unfortunately, there was no one to throw it to. F. McKnight Wakeley played first base as though he were on parade and wore his glove backwards on the wrong hand. Gum and Emmett O'Dell made fewer errors than anyone except Pennylegion.

In the outfield, Valentini, now playing Ammerman's position, accounted for a few outs on easy fly balls, but Taz and Morgan were an athletic detriment to the team, until Morgan made his decisive play. At the top of the fourth, score 32 to 4, an ox-like sanitation worker with muscles bulging from years of throwing garbage over the side walls and backs of high trucks, smashed a line drive into the unprotected mid-section of Alderman Morgan who, at the time, was looking at something in the sky. The thump was heard back at the pavilion. Morgan Morgan sat down heavily and threw up on his plus fours.

Everyone ran to the outfield to make sure Alderman Morgan was all right—including the garbageman who had hit the pitched baseball. Morgan recovered almost immediately, physically unharmed, but Umpire Henry Plain decided it was best to end the ball game without further chance of injury.

As the crowd started to drift away from the baseball diamond, Zulp materialized beside Tretheway.

"Where's Wan Ho?" Zulp whispered hoarsely in Tretheway's ear.

"Eh?" Tretheway jumped.

"I think we've got our man."

"What?"

"Dammit, Tretheway! Our man. The killer."

"Who?" Tretheway tried desperately to second-guess the Chief. Mac and Jake leaned forward. Ammerman remained seated on the grass.

"Constable." Zulp looked at Jake. "Arrest that man."

"What man?" Jake asked.

Zulp surreptitiously jerked his head in the direction of the shuffling crowd. "That one."

"Which one?"

"The big one, dammit!" Zulp said impatiently. "The one that struck down Morgan."

"Hold on." Tretheway saw Wan Ho in the crowd and beckoned him over. "I'll stop him if necessary. How do you know he's the one?"

"Didn't you see him attack Morgan?" Zulp asked.

"With a softball?" Tretheway said.

Wan Ho entered the circle. "Can I help?"

When Wan Ho heard Zulp's off-the-cuff theory of the garbage-man's premeditated attack on an elected official, he took a deep breath and explained why such a conclusion was unlikely.

"Nobody, not even a professional ball player, is that accurate with a ball and bat. And from that distance, a blow in the stomach, especially with a softball, would never be lethal. And another thing," Wan Ho continued, "if Morgan had been on his toes, nothing would've happened. He would've caught it or got the hell out of the way."

Zulp, undaunted, wore what he considered a knowing look. "Here's the clincher." He lowered his voice confidentially. "I happen to know, from a source I can't reveal" (Zulp's well-known source was a sycophantic washroom attendant who had dreams of becoming a City Hall elevator operator with white gloves) "that the garbagemen have it in for the politicians."

"Surely not enough to murder?" Tretheway reasoned.

Jake nodded in the background. Mac showed interest.

"Well . . ." Zulp hesitated.

"And what about the twenty-fourth?" Wan Ho came to the rescue.

"The what?"

"The twenty-fourth of August. St. Bartholomew's Day."

"You're right." Zulp remembered. Tretheway and Wan Ho exchanged relieved smiles. "You're right," Zulp repeated. He slammed his fist into his palm. "Nothing'll happen today. Damn fine mental exercise, though. Keeps everyone on their toes." Zulp walked away. "Stimulating!"

Tretheway was first to find his voice. "Hard to believe."

"Could've been nasty," Wan Ho said.

"An attempted murder charge," Mac said.

"With a softball," Jake said.

"At fifty yards," Tretheway said.

"Can you imagine what the Toronto papers would've done with that?" Wan Ho asked.

"Did I miss anything?" Ammerman stood up.

"It's time to eat, Harold," Tretheway said.

It was almost six o'clock. Everyone wandered back to his table, car, piece of grass or wherever he'd decided to enjoy supper. The city, through the generosity of taxpayers, supplied free hot dogs and pop to anyone who looked sixteen or under, while the adults looked after themselves.

Tretheway made short work of Addie's cold chicken. "Great, Addie." He then table-hopped and sampled everything from cabbage rolls to kosher corned beef, from homemade dandelion wine to bubbly burgundy.

"Eat up, Tretheway!" Zulp shouted at him across the tables. "We need all the weight we can get!" Tretheway smiled back, not too broadly, and returned to his own table for dessert.

Zulp had referred to what was perhaps the high spot of the day if you were a fireman or policeman: the tug-o-war. It wasn't a big event, really, unless you were a participant, but over the years it had become the pivotal point of the picnic. Parents waited to see it before they carried their sleepy children down to the ferry dock or to their cars. Teenagers past the age of eating sandwiches with their picnicking parents arrived in time to see it before the dance started. Everyone watched it. And the *Expositor* always ran a picture of the winners in the Monday edition.

By the time the shadows had lengthened and the entertainment committee was thinking about hanging lanterns in the pavilion, the crowd had swelled to its largest for the day. They formed a loose, elliptical shape around the area prepared for the contest. A shallow, circular pit had been dug earlier by the Works Department and filled with water (now muddy) from Old Number Thirteen Pumper (Ret.). The crowd waited to see which losing team would be dragged through the mire.

The gladiators pushed their way through the crowd to boisterous cheering. They had changed into their new T-shirts, paid for by themselves, which added a professional touch to the show. The firemen's shirts were bright red with the words "SMOKE EATERS" emblazoned across their chests in yellow and orange flames, while the policemen wore a conservative blue style carrying the words "SQUARE JOHNS" in no-nonsense sans serif letters. Tretheway was the anchor man for the police. His XL T-shirt still showed a generous amount of bare stomach.

The teams lined up on either side of the brackish water. Tretheway slipped into the fixed loop spliced into the end of the rope and felt it course roughly over his right shoulder, down his back, under his other arm and return, following the contour of his stomach. The heavy hemp rope, although two inches in diameter, looked no stronger in his grip than a substantial skipping rope. In front of him, the other team members spaced themselves down its length.

Mayor Phinneas "Fireball" Trutt, the official referee, stood to one side and carefully watched the golden tassle hanging over the water that marked the exact centre of the rope.

"Make ready to pull," he shouted.

The rope tightened as both teams leaned backward. Tretheway dug his heels in; so did the large fireman at the opposite end. The tassle moved slowly back and forth. Trutt raised his starter's pistol in the air, his eyes fixed on the golden marker.

"Wait for it," he said quietly, but everybody heard him in the hush. "Wait for it . . ."

He fired the pistol. All hell broke loose.

Air blew violently from twenty pair of lungs. The crowd shrieked. For ten long minutes, the rope remained as straight as a poker and moved no more than six inches either way. The participants grunted explosively. Their track shoes scored the earth. The rope creaked. Sweat stained the new T-shirts. Painful muscular grimaces replaced scowls. Sinews, unused since last year, stood out like ropes themselves.

Gradually, ever so gradually, the first fireman slid toward the water. Increased efforts on behalf of the Smoke Eaters stopped the advance, but only for a moment. The partisan crowd around the police end of the rope sensed a swing in their favour and cheered louder. Tretheway pulled harder in response. The first fireman was inches from the water when the Smoke Eaters stopped the slide with desperate back-pedalling. After another moment of strained immobility, the first policeman slid toward the water. Cheers rose at the other end. Tretheway felt the renewed aggression through the rope and, somehow over the tumult, heard Addie shout.

"Pull, Albert! Pull!"

When Tretheway heard Addie shout out his first name for all to hear, he called on his reserve strength the way a thirsty camel calls on his stored water supply. Slowly, as though shifting to a low gear, he pumped his huge legs and pulled backwards. Fireman Number One slipped into the water; followed by Number Two. Number Three's heels skidded into the pond. The policemen had victory in their grasp.

There are times when a small sound will intrude upon someone's senses under any circumstances simply because it's out of place; because the sound shouldn't be there—like the tinkle of breaking glass during a deep sleep; like a baby crying in a business office; like thunder in the midst of a raging blizzard. Thretheway heard an avalanche of paper.

From his viewpoint, he could see over the tug-o-war teams and spectators to where the mountain of newspaper was silhouetted in the low rays of sun. Tretheway thought he saw a head, strangely pointed, or figures, maybe two or three, at the top of the pile. He thought he saw movement there also. Tretheway noticed Jake and other policemen, who were supposed to be part of the Master Plan, cheering their heads off. And he realized that at least four of the police tug-o-war team were bodyguards. He couldn't see Mac, Pennylegion, Ammerman or Bartholomew Gum. In fact, except for Mayor Trutt, who was holding the pistol in the air and trying to look non-partisan despite the firemen's imminent defeat, Tretheway couldn't see any Council members at all. Less than a second elapsed from the time he heard the paper avalanche to the time he made his move.

Tretheway lurched forward and jumped out of the loop. He jogged toward the newspaper pile. The people in front of him appeared to be frozen. To Tretheway, they seemed paralyzed. Their hands were raised, but not moving; their mouths open, but not cheering. Tretheway stopped in front of Jake.

"Where's Mac?" he shouted.

"E . . . eh . . .?" Jake stammered.

"Mac! Controller MacCulla! Where the hell is he?"

"I . . . I don't know."

"What's going on, Albert?" Addie asked.

"You're supposed to know!" Tretheway shouted at Jake. "Let's go!"

Tretheway, with Jake right behind, pushed his way through the crowd, taking precious seconds to lift children, and sometimes adults, out of his path. Behind him, if he had taken the time to look, the last of the betrayed police tug-o-war team was slithering through the mud hole. The perplexed but jubilant firemen were falling back on themselves with the sudden and unexpected victory. Mayor Trutt, no longer able to contain his firehouse sympathies, emptied the starter's pistol in the air to celebrate the Smoke Eater win. Chief Zulp was not so happy.

"Tretheway!" Zulp shouted. "Tretheway!" His cries were lost in the uproar. "Stop that man! He's a deserter!"

"Where are we going?" Jake shouted at Tretheway's back.

"Paper!" Tretheway pointed. "Pile of paper!"

"What?"

"Just follow me."

When they reached the edge of the crowd, Tretheway broke into a gallop. Jake followed. They ran around to the other side of the newspaper mountain. Tretheway stopped and scanned the pile.

"There's no one here." At the base of the pile Tretheway noticed a lumpy, uneven section as though some bundles had shifted. "Dig!" He tossed bundles of newspaper aside like bits of balsa wood.

"What?" Jake asked.

"Dig! Dammit, dig!"

Jake, convinced Tretheway had damaged something in his reasoning process during the tug-o-war, started to dig anyway. More people arrived, including Zulp.

"Tretheway," Zulp began. "Have you gone mad? Nine wet and filthy comrades. Lying back there. In the muck. What the hell happened?" He ducked a bundle of newspapers that came in his direction.

"What are you looking for?"

"Don't ask."

"Eh?"

"Get some help."

Zulp opened his mouth to shout but changed his mind. He turned toward the crowd. "Get some more men in here. Quickly!"

For five minutes the men laboured wordlessly while whispered rumours spread efficiently through the curious crowd. They found nothing. Tretheway began to wonder whether he had seen anything in the first place; the shadows could have been just shadows or a trick played by the setting sun; wind could have caused the avalanche. Doubt slid under the door of Tretheway's confidence. He straightened up.

"Tretheway," Zulp began. "How sure are you . . ."

"Inspector."

"Don't interrupt," Zulp said.

"Inspector," Jake repeated. "There's something here."

Tretheway walked over. The others pushed closer.

"Give me a hand, Jake." Tretheway and Jake cleared several bundles of newspaper from the body. The crowd became quiet. Some early arrivals from the RFYLI Brass Band tuned up in the pavilion.

"It's a child," someone in the crowd said.

Tretheway gently rolled the body over. The beautiful features of Henry Plain faced the darkening sky.

"Shall I get Doc Nooner?" Jake asked.

"Yes," Tretheway said. "But there's no hurry."

When Doc Nooner arrived he confirmed Tretheway's opinion. "Nothing you could've done. Death by suffocation," he said, after a cursory but experienced examination. "What the hell was he doing up there, anyway?"

Zulp glared at Tretheway. "Do you know anything about this?"

"Perhaps I should clear the air . . ." Tretheway began.

"That'd be nice," Zulp encouraged.

Tretheway went on to explain why he had left the tug-o-war so suddenly. He told about the figures or shadows at the top of the pile.

"Did you actually see anyone?" Zulp asked.

"I think so."

"Think? That's just great. Aren't you sure? Could you identify anyone?"

"Not really," Tretheway said. "And at that distance even if I saw . . ."

"If?"

"I'm afraid so."

Wan Ho entered the conversation. "You mean, it could've been Henry Plain by himself that you saw?"

"It's possible," Tretheway admitted. "But it still doesn't explain why he was up there."

"To get a better view of the proceedings," Zulp said. "You know how short he was."

Tretheway grimaced. "I doubt that."

"Dammit, Tretheway! There's no evidence to support foul play."

Tretheway sulked.

Zulp turned to the Doctor. "Nor any medical evidence either. That right, Nooner?"

"I guess so. Some bruises again. Nothing conclusive."

"Well, then." Zulp took a deep breath. "Okay. Let's not panic. Cool heads. It's a tragedy. But he had been drinking. Wine. Warm day. Where's Mrs Plain?"

"She's with Addie and some of the other women," Jake said.

"Good. Best not bother her. Let's wrap it up. Call it a day. Nasty day." Zulp walked away. "Nasty."

No one objected. There wasn't much anyone could do. Even if there was a killer out there somewhere, Tretheway thought, it would be fruitless to search for him now. It was getting dark. Hundreds of people were milling about. Where would you look? he asked himself. And who or what would you look for?

Later that evening, Tretheway, Jake and Fred sat on their back porch and enjoyed, as much as they were able to under the circumstances, the star-filled, balmy night. They had rehashed the day, from parking the car to the dance cancellation, including Tretheway's possible sighting of pointy-headed people, but nothing helpful had come to the surface. Henry Plain was resting at a convenient local undertaker while his shocked family had been billeted with friends. Everyone had left LaSalle Park by ten o'clock except for five policemen stationed at the paper pile. They were there to prevent another tragedy and to preserve any evidence for daylight scrutiny.

"It could've been an accident," Jake said.

"I don't think so," Tretheway said.

"But Zulp said . . ."

Tretheway glared at Jake. Jake didn't finish. Tretheway took a six-ounce pull on his quart of Molson. He repositioned his upper body and belched.

"It fits too well."

"Hm?"

"The head civil servant. On Civic Holiday. Smothered in paper. Too pat."

"When you put it that way . . ."

"He could've been lured behind that pile. Chased up it. Head forced into a bundle. Held there. By one or more persons. Then the avalanche."

"All conjecture."

"True." Tretheway watched a firefly buzz around his stockinged feet. "I liked Henry."

"So did I."

Tretheway waved the fly away. "He never hurt anybody."

"What are we going to do?"

"Go to bed." Tretheway stood up and stretched. "At least, that's what I'm going to do."

On their way through the kitchen, Tretheway grabbed two quarts of beer from the ice box in the the fingers of one hand. The bottles clinked together as he mounted the stairs.

On August 24, St. Bartholomew's Day, Chief Zulp, or at least Mrs Zulp, informed the switchboard at Central Police Station that her husband would not be in to work.

"He has a slight temperature and a nasty cough. Touch of the flu. Nothing serious, but I think he should spend the day in bed. No," she said in answer to the switchboard's question. "He can't take any calls. Surely you can get by for one day."

Alderman Bartholomew Gum received no extra guards or care on August 24. The day passed without mishap.

SEPTEMBER

Two things made the September murder different from the others. First, it was unexpected. Second, they caught the murderer red-handed. Or, at least, Chief Zulp said they did.

The month started sensibly enough for the season. Sunday dawned warm and sunny. Higher humidity and showers were predicted for later in the week. Fort York football fans were optimistic about their beloved FY Taggers demolishing the hated Toronto Argonauts in the traditional Labour Day game. Most of the people who had summer cottages were back in the city. Schools opened on Tuesday. So, except for the war news (the Battle of Britain was just beginning) it was a normal start for September.

The Labour Day parade began early Monday morning. It was less militaristic than the Dominion Day parade, but there were just as many uniforms in evidence. The politicians who disagreed with Zulp's theory of accidental death in the Henry Plain affair were influential enough to demand, and get, extra police protection, especially on another holiday.

All off-duty regular policemen had been called in, a detachment of Ontario Provincial Police was actually marching in the parade, extra Military Police lined the route and the Federal Government, with the idea that one Mountie could still quell an Indian uprising, sent one Royal Canadian Mounted Police (RCMP) Constable.

The main body of the parade was made up of hard core labour. They were unmilitarily jolly and marched out of step, but their raucous banter gave a sort of industrial Mardi Gras flavour to the procession.

Once again, Mayor Trutt took the salute in front of the City Hall. Labour, military, police, Scouts, Marion Day celebrants, CWACS, Six Nation Indians and others he couldn't identify filed past Trutt's sincere, hat-over-the-heart gesture without incident. At the finish of the parade, most of the participants enjoyed a cold cuts and beer lunch—courtesy of the FY Labour Council—

before they attended the football game (Fort York triumphed over Toronto in a boring, one-sided match).

While the city held its collective breath, Labour Day drew to a close in every union hall across the city's wards without a report of homicide.

By the time Tuesday was half over, most Fort York inhabitants hoped with all their hearts that Henry Plain's death had been accidental. They hoped that, for some reason, the St. Swithin's Day drowning was the end of it; the finish to the strange chain of events that had plagued Fort York.

There was a slight scare at the end of the first week. A *FY Expositor* reporter mentioned to Chief Zulp that Rosh Hashanah, the start of the Jewish New Year, and Yom Kippur, the Day of Atonement, both fell sometime in September. Before this could be properly researched, Zulp dispatched a Flying Squad (his substitute for the abandoned Master Plan) to the home of Harold Ammerman, the only Jewish member of Council. Four cruisers, sirens screaming, emptied eight policemen onto the Alderman's front lawn. They came close to causing another political fatality by bursting into the old gentleman's home and shaking him out of a deep nap. It was Ammerman himself who explained to the protectors that the Jewish holidays started in October this year. This was explained later to Zulp. The *Expositor* reporter couldn't be reached.

As each day of September passed, the inhabitants of Fort York grew more optimistic. They endured Maryland Day, September 12, the anniversary of the defense of that city in the War of 1812. Nothing happened. The fifteenth was Independence Day for Central America. A small number of Costa Ricans, wearing gaily-coloured native costumes, jiggled around on the City Hall steps at noon for about five minutes. But nothing happened. The occasion, rather than the holiday, of American Constitution Day, September 15, went slowly through its twenty-four hours. Chilean Independence Day came and departed unnoticed on the eighteenth. A few Anglican churches celebrated the Feast of St. Matthew on the twenty-first. But it was very orderly and religious. Nothing happened.

So by Saturday night, the twenty-eighth, most people went to their beds feeling that the crisis was past. The next morning, however, something happened.

"Beautiful Sunday for your walk, Albert." Addie bustled about the kitchen. It was early for Tretheway (7:30) but Addie had been up for the last hour cleaning the kitchen after Saturday night's euchre session. She had also made breakfast already for O. Pitts who had an early sermon practice.

Tretheway looked out of the back window. "Always nice after a rain." He stretched his arms over his head, lifting the 2nd Life Guards' crest on his sweat shirt a foot and a half. "Flowers look good. Specially the daisies."

"They should, Albert." Addie threw the day-old cigar butts into the garbage pail. Tretheway wouldn't let her throw them out the same night. "Particularly today."

Tretheway stopped in mid-stretch. He had the sudden, spooky feeling that he didn't want Addie to go on.

"Ah . . . today?"

"Yes."

"What's so special about today?"

"You know what kind of daisies they are?"

"Yes. Michaelmas daisies. What about it?"

"Today is Michaelmas Day."

Tretheway shivered in the warm sunlight.

At about the time Tretheway shivered, O. Pitts discovered, to his surprise, that the front door of University Hall was unlocked. He entered and stood for a moment in the silence. Hearing nothing more alarming than the characteristic complaints and creaks of an old empty building, O. Pitts advanced down the spacious hall and paused again outside the heavy double doors of the chapel. The soft coo of a mourning dove startled him. He pushed quickly through the doors.

Once inside, he was comforted by the familiar surroundings. Warm oak panelling lined the walls. Tall, leaded Gothic windows, sculptured replicas of Baptist Saints glared down on polished wooden pews built to contain a repentant congregation. O. Pitts took pleasure in the orderly fashion in which the rows of seats marched toward the front of the chapel, stopping just before a small stage and a single large stained-glass window. Ordinarily, the stage held a lectern or, as his professors called it, a practice pulpit, but today he saw two persons there, one seated, the other lying down. O. Pitts blinked.

"Hello. Who's there, please?"

He squinted towards the stage. No one answered. O. Pitts stepped on something soft. He jumped back. Looking down, he saw several purple flowers, daisies with yellow centres, scattered over the floor. His gaze followed more daisies down the aisle and onto the stage. He inched his way toward the strange twosome.

"Do I know you?"

Still nobody answered.

When O. Pitts got close enough to stop squinting, he saw that the man sitting on a chair had a large sword in his grip. The blade was stained a deep red and appeared charred. For the first time, O. Pitts noticed the acrid smell of smoke. He switched his attention to the man flat on his back. It was obvious, even to O. Pitts, that the man was dead. Congealed blood from what looked like a stab wound in the stomach covered the area around the body. The shirt around the wound was badly stained.

"Who . . . who . . ." O. Pitts stammered.

Alderman Morgan Morgan rose and pointed the sword at Lucifer Taz, his fallen comrade. "Lucifer," he whispered. "Lucifer . . ." Morgan sat down again.

O. Pitts' eyes lifted to the stained-glass window in the background. It depicted St. Michael, greatest of the Archangels, a glory round his head, in a suit of shining armour with his flaming sword raised to the heavens. The fallen Devil lay at his feet.

"Shit," O. Pitts said.

At the very same time Tretheway was listening to Addie explain the legend of Michaelmas Day, O. Pitts pulled himself together enough to scream and run outside the chapel to call for help. When his index finger steadied down long enough to dial the operator, he called the police; then the Tretheway household. As luck would have it, Zulp was the first one to arrive in a Flying Squad car. He sized up the situation immediately.

"Alderman Morgan. You're under arrest."

Morgan hadn't moved since O. Pitts had fled. He still sat clutching the stained sword and didn't appear to have heard Zulp.

"Did you hear me, Morgan?"

Morgan turned toward the voice. Questioning wrinkles lined his forehead. He didn't speak.

"Constable. Disarm that man," Zulp ordered. "I don't think he's quite right."

Morgan gave no resistance. He handed the sword over to a

policeman when asked and followed him obediently to a quiet corner of the chapel, where he sat for the next half hour—still without speaking—while the investigation proceeded.

As it worked out, Zulp was correct about Morgan not being quite right. Dr Nooner confirmed this. He arrived shortly after Tretheway and Jake. Wan Ho and a small army of investigators, fingerprint men, photographers and uniformed men who were no longer the novelty they had been on Father's Day, made up the group.

"Shock. Severe shock," Nooner said. "Some sort of traumatic experience . . ."

"Like killing someone?" Zulp interrupted.

"Possible. Resulting in a loss of speech. Probably temporary."

"But he has to answer some questions."

"He can't talk."

"Hm. Awkward. When will he be all right?"

"Can't say. He should be in the hospital."

"Yes. Quite right. Just a formality anyway."

"Sir?" Tretheway entered the conversation.

"Well, we all know what he's done," Zulp explained.

"You mean this killing?" Tretheway said. "Lucifer Taz's murder?"

"Certainly." Zulp clasped his hands behind his back and began to rock back and forth. "On the scene. Murder weapon in his hand. Covered with blood. Too shocked by what he's done to escape. Incoherent. No doubt about it."

"What about the other murders?" Tretheway asked.

"I would think so. Yes. He's the one. My opinion."

"But what about the motive?"

"Come, come, Tretheway. I know we don't have all the facts. But I'm sure there's a motive out there." Zulp gestured toward the bustling policemen. "Somewhere. Don't be afraid to admit the old Chief was a step or two ahead of you. Eh? Unless you have a more likely candidate?"

"Not really."

"Well then. That's settled. Don't worry about it." Zulp frowned suddenly. "What are you doing here anyway? How did you find out about this?"

"O. Pitts," Tretheway said.

"What?"

"O. Pitts," Jake explained. "The student who found Taz and Morgan. He boards with us."

"He called us," Tretheway said. "Wouldn't say what it was over the phone. Just said to get here."

"Oh. All right. I suppose." Zulp shook his head. "Back to work. Good thing to have over. Have people sleep in their beds again. Safely." He strode toward the investigating group already capably headed by Sergeant Wan Ho.

"Walk us to the car, will you, Doc?" Tretheway said.

"Sure thing." Dr Nooner yawned. "I'm going back to bed anyhow."

The three of them went down the stairs and out into the fresh sunlight. They skirted a group of early worshippers. Pious, indignant shock fought with excitement for control of their expressions, while a professor explained why the morning service was cancelled. The trio stopped at Jake's Pontiac.

"Nice car, Jake," Dr Nooner said.

"Looks good with the top down," Jake said.

"What year?"

" 'Thirty-three. Seven years old."

"Great shape."

"I look after it."

"Did the sword kill him?" Tretheway said louder than conversational level.

"What?" Dr Nooner said.

"The sword!" Tretheway flaunted his disinterest in cars by continuing his interruption. "Is it the murder weapon?"

"Ah . . . I think so," Dr Nooner answered. "Can't say for sure but it looks like it."

"Where'd it come from?"

Nooner shook his head.

"Probably from the school," Jake suggested. FYU was Jake's alma mater. "There are three or four suits of armour around the University. I'll wager one's without a sword."

"Right." Tretheway accepted Jake's explanation. "And the burn marks are from the sword."

"Just like Addie said," Jake agreed.

"Probably dipped in gasoline." Tretheway nodded. "Although if I know Morgan and Taz, it was probably brandy."

"Would you two please tell me what the hell's going on?" Dr Nooner demanded.

"The legend of Michaelmas," Tretheway said. "Didn't you notice the stained glass window?"

"What about it?"

"That's St. Michael," Tretheway explained, the story fresh in his mind from Addie's telling. "He's honoured on Michaelmas Day. September 29. Yesterday. He's the greatest Angel of the Lord. Delivered the commandments to Moses. Knows the secret of creation. And he's mentioned in the Book of Revelations. There was a war in heaven. The Archangel Michael and all his angel friends cast out the Devil and his followers. And this is how he's usually shown. With his flaming sword smiting the Devil. Or . . ." Tretheway held up a fat finger for emphasis, "as we sometimes call him, Lucifer."

"I'll be damned," Dr Nooner said.

"What about the flowers?" Jake asked.

"Symbolic. Michaelmas daisies. Named after the same St. Michael. Once again, neat. A pattern."

"Except for one thing," Dr Nooner said.

"Eh?" Tretheway asked. Jake raised his eyebrows.

"This time the killer was caught."

Tretheway's thin lips pursed together.

"Well, he *was* caught. Red-handed, too," Dr Nooner continued. "Surely there's no doubt in your mind . . ."

"It looks bad, all right," Tretheway admitted.

"Bad?" Dr Nooner blurted. "More than bad. Sitting there with the sword. Time of death is right."

"Hang on." Tretheway quieted the doctor by the tone of his voice. He waved his finger in the air again. "Justice. Innocent until proven otherwise. His actions for last night will have to be checked. What was his motive? And what about the other murders?"

"This is the one he'll be tried for," Dr Nooner persisted.

"I know," Tretheway agreed. "All the same, if he's found guilty, wouldn't you feel more comfortable if he's placed at the scene of the others?"

"I guess so," Dr Nooner admitted.

"I'd feel a lot better," Jake said.

"And I want to hear his side of it," Tretheway said. "A confession would be better than him playing the clam."

"You can't tell when he'll talk, I guess," Jake asked the doctor.

"Not for sure, Jake. I'm sure he'll come round. Maybe tomorrow. Or next month. Maybe another good shock'll do it." Dr Nooner started for his car. "Let's hope it's all over."

"See you, Doc," Jake said.

"Let's go, Jake." Tretheway lowered himself into the passenger seat of Jake's car.

"Right." Jake slipped into the smooth leather seat behind the wheel. He pushed the starter button and let the engine idle while he adjusted the choke.

"You suppose Addie knows about this?" Tretheway said.

"I doubt it."

"Who's going to tell her?"

Jake pulled the gear shift noiselessly into first. "Well, I suppose . . . maybe I . . ."

"Good boy, Jake."

OCTOBER

Fort York settled down to normal, if wartime, living. The invasion of England was not considered imminent, as it was two months before; the war savings bond drive was going well; the practice blackouts were successful—more fun than frightening—and gas rationing, food shortages and meatless Tuesdays were becoming accepted facts of life.

An early cold snap accelerated the changing colours of the leaves. The lush green of late summer turned magically to gold, orange or scarlet in the metamorphosis of another year. V's of Canada geese became common sights in the fall skies. And the time for giving thanks drew near.

With the news of the Holiday Killer's (*FY Expositor* journalese) capture, the emotional pendulum of Fort York's citizenry swung back past the norm to the point where everyone, perhaps too fervently, expected worry-free holidays from now on; almost everyone.

"When's Thanksgiving this year?" Addie asked.

"Fourteenth, Addie," Jake said. "A week next Monday."

The two of them were sitting in the warm fragrance of Addie's comfortable kitchen, sipping tea and watching Tretheway out in the back yard trying to send Fred home.

Since suppertime, Tretheway had been uprooting frost-killed plants and foliage for his compost heap. Fred the Labrador had followed him all over the garden. She sat down to watch while he tore out offending growth and trotted at his heels when he carried an accumulation of these future nutrients to the fenced-in pile. Tretheway had spoken kindly to the dog and even patted her head once or twice during the evening, but when the air turned cool and crisp in the waning light, he thought it was time to go in. He stood now, like an ancient and noble statue, pointing theatrically to his neighbour's back yard. Fred sat at his feet, unmoving. From where Jake and Addie sat, they could make out the futile commands forming on Tretheway's lips.

"You can tell that dog's not a policeman," Jake said.

"Or a relative," Addie added.

They shared a giggle.

Tretheway sprinted suddenly toward the back porch. The dog followed. Tretheway took the steps three at a time, slipped nimbly through the screen door and slammed it quickly behind him. Fred thumped solidly into the lower wooden half. Addie and Jake looked disapprovingly at each other. When Tretheway turned and came into the kitchen, he was whistling silently.

Jake and Addie picked up where they'd left off.

"Then what's today?" Addie asked.

"Friday. The fourth," Jake said.

"The Feast of St. Francis of Assisi," Tretheway said. He turned on both taps at the kitchen sink.

"St. Francis of Assisi?" Addie repeated.

"Feast? Never heard of it," Jake said.

Tretheway rinsed the rich loam from his hands. "And you probably didn't know that Missouri Day was the first Monday in October. That's the seventh."

"No. Not really." Jake wrinkled his brow at Addie.

"And how about the ninth? Wednesday." Tretheway dried his hands on a couple of Addie's flowered tea towels. Addie frowned.

"You have your choice of two," Tretheway continued. "Feast of St. Denis, patron saint of France. Or Leif Ericson Day. That's got a nice ring to it. Landed in Vineland about 1000 A.D. The very day before Chinese Independence Day. That's the tenth. Then Columbus Day two days later."

"Albert," Addie interrupted, "what are you going on about?"

"That's my list. My holiday list for October."

"But we don't have to worry about those holidays." Addie looked worried. "Do we?"

"You're right, Addie," Tretheway said. "We don't have to worry about them. And I'll bet money we can enjoy Thanksgiving weekend. Also Yorktown Day on the nineteenth. And did you know there's another bloody feast coming on the twenty-fourth for another bloody Archangel? St. Raphael." Tretheway felt in his pocket for a cigar. Addie frowned again, this time at Tretheway's language, but pointed to a humidor on the kitchen counter. Tretheway grunted and took a cigar.

"Did you also know that someone called St. Crispin and his

brother have a feast on the next day? You know what they're the patron saint of? Shoemakers!" Tretheway looked at Jake. "Is there anyone on Council that's a shoemaker?" He felt for a match. This time, Jake pointed at a large box beside the humidor. Tretheway took one and easily struck it on the top of the door jamb. He puffed deeply several times without inhaling. It seemed to soothe him.

"American Navy Day on the twenty-eighth we can forget. And I can't get too worked up about Czechoslovakian Independence Day, the twenty-eighth."

"You say we don't have to worry about those holidays, Albert?" Addie said.

"Not if Morgan's the guilty one," Jake said.

"Whether he's guilty or not, Jake," Tretheway said. "It doesn't matter."

"I don't quite follow," Jake said.

"If he is guilty," Tretheway explained, "obviously nothing'll happen on those holidays. But if he isn't guilty . . ."

"Oh, Albert," Addie said. Jake laid his hand on her generously-sized shoulder.

"Take it easy, Addie," Tretheway said. "But all we found out is that Morgan was at a party with most of the city fathers on Saturday. He and Lucifer Taz left together at about midnight. We don't know what happened from that point on until O. Pitts found them."

Jake nodded in agreement.

"Now I'm just supposing," Tretheway went on. "But supposing the killer got a phenomenal break? Suppose Morgan blundered into the picture at just the wrong moment? Everybody says he's the killer. The chase is off. The real killer's out of danger. He can pick any holiday he wants."

"I thought he always did," Jake said.

"Not really," Tretheway said. "Think back." He was leaning backwards against the counter, facing Jake and Addie, arms folded, puffing on his cigar. An ash fell on a wrinkle of his green sweat shirt in between the words "City of Verdun" and "Hammer Throw Champion." "The first three were pranks. Done on obvious holidays. Valentine's, St. Patrick's Day and April Fool's. Firecracker Day, though more serious, much the same thing. June, Father's Day, the first serious one. But still a fairly obvious holiday. Right?"

Jake nodded. Addie just stared and looked uncomfortable.

"So now," Tretheway continued, "everybody is on guard. Everybody's second guessing about July. What's the obvious holiday? The first. Dominion Day. But what happened? Nothing. When did he strike? St. Swithin's Day. A surprise." Another ash fell onto Tretheway's stomach. "Threw everybody off balance. Nobody knew what to expect for August. Some obscure Saint's Day again? No! He hammers us right on Civic Holiday."

"You don't think that was an accident?" Jake asked.

Tretheway shook his head. "No. It was a perfect set-up. Inviting. All those people. The excitement. It wasn't an accident." He held up his hand to stop Jake from interrupting. "I know what Zulp said. All that did was help the killer. Took the pressure off."

Tretheway puffed on his cigar and plowed on. "Remember Labour Day? Everyone half expecting something to happen? When it was all over, they relaxed. Then he gets us on Michaelmas Day." Tretheway shook his head. "Michaelmas Day. Hardly a popular holiday."

"So in October?" Jake asked. "I mean, if . . ."

Addie frowned.

"October?" Tretheway recrossed his arms. "I think it would've been Navy Day. Or Chinese Independence Day. Or whatever. But not now. Not if the killer's still running free. With nothing to fear. He'll pick the obvious holiday." Tretheway took several small puffs, then plucked the cigar from his mouth and pushed away from the counter. All the ashes fell from his shirt to the floor. "Hallowe'en," he said with confidence.

"Oh, dear," Addie said crossly. "I wish you wouldn't do that."

She was upset only partly because of the ashes on her clean floor, but, like most of the citizens of Fort York, Addie wanted to believe that the murders were solved, over with, a thing of the past. If Morgan was guilty, she reasoned, she could sleep nights and enjoy holidays once again. Addie had pushed the thought of more violence into the dark corners of her mind; when Tretheway had prodded it out into the bright light of possibility, she was scared and resented it.

"I'm sorry, Addie," Tretheway said. "But don't forget it's still guesswork. Just thinking out loud again."

"I don't care," Addie said. "It's still upsetting."

"I know, Addie." Jake reassured her. "Ninety-nine chances out of a hundred nothing'll happen."

"I wish Alderman Morgan would say something," Addie said.

"So do I," Jake said.

"I've been thinking about that," Tretheway said. "Maybe we could help matters along."

"Oh," Jake said. "Like what?"

"Remember what Doc Nooner said about another shock?"

"Ah, yes," Jake said.

"Albert," Addie said. "You're not going to do anything you shouldn't, are you?"

"Addie, don't be silly." Tretheway came over and sat down beside Jake. "Between the two of us, do you think we could build a device with some sort of wrecking ball that swung back and forth? Like a pendulum. And it would advance slowly toward some object? Eventually smashing it?"

"I don't know," Jake said. "I'd have to know a little more about it."

"One thing," Tretheway added. "It would have to be obvious that the object, whatever it may be, was going to be destroyed."

"When do you need it?"

"Hallowe'en."

Addie rose abruptly and pushed her way out through the swinging door of the kitchen. "Friday night," she said. " 'Hollywood Hotel' is on." She headed for the radio in the parlour. Addie loved Frank Parker.

The rest of the month passed just about the way Tretheway had said it would. From St. Francis of Assisi's Feast to Czech Independence Day, the city lived through all the obscure holidays Trctheway had researched, without a hint, an attempt, or deed of murder. Thus the case against Morgan Morgan was strengthened.

Of all the holidays, Thanksgiving was the only one celebrated to any extent in Fort York. It fell on the fourteenth. Schools and businesses were closed, most families enjoyed a turkey dinner, thanks were offered for bounty and prayers were said in churches and homes for the men and boys gone to war.

There was another traditional, back-to-back scheduling of football games, this time against the Montreal Allouettes. The Fort York Taggers lost on Saturday but scored eighteen unanswered points to redeem themselves on the Thanksgiving Monday. Jake and Addie went to the game while Tretheway—holding the opinion that football was only slightly less sissy than baseball—decided to stay home and work on his device.

He and Jake had worked off and on, like two Bolshevik conspirators in a B-movie, almost every evening in October, building, tearing down, rebuilding, until, after many harsh oaths and bruised thumbs, a Rube Goldberg-type of structure stood in the dusty cellar. It was referred to by Tretheway and Jake as, simply, The Machine. In the fourth week of October, somewhere between Yorktown Day and the Feast of St. Crispin, Tretheway and Jake decided to run a test.

"Addie!" Tretheway shouted upstairs. "Come and look for a minute."

Tretheway and Jake stared upwards at the cellar rafters and followed the sounds of Addie's footsteps to the top of the stairs. The cellar door opened.

"Albert," Addie shouted sweetly in a voice she used when there were unexpected guests in the parlour, "we have visitors."

"That's all right," Tretheway shouted back. He stopped himself abruptly from saying more and moved quickly but quietly to the foot of the stairs. "Who?" he whispered.

Addie bent over and whispered back. "Bartholomew Gum and old Mr Ammerman."

Tretheway resumed his normal voice. "Fine. Bring them down." He returned to The Machine.

"Jake, let's try the milk this time. Probably be more spectacular."

"Right." Jake placed an unopened quart bottle of milk at the business end of The Machine and clamped it in tightly.

This time, three sets of footsteps made their way to the cellar door. Addie led the way.

"Watch your heads, gentlemen."

Bartholomew Gum and Harold Ammerman followed her downstairs. As ward four Aldermen, they were visiting Addie on official business. Addie sat on the neighbourhood Community Council. The three had been discussing the parade, individual and group prizes, refreshments and general logistics of the annual children's Hallowe'en party when Tretheway had interrupted them from the cellar. They all gathered around The Machine.

"Impressive." Ammerman nodded wisely.

"What is it?" Gum looked at Ammerman. "Do you know what it is?"

"Impressive," Ammerman repeated.

Tretheway turned to Jake. "Bottle secure?"

Jake nodded. Tretheway faced his puzzled audience.

"If you'll just bear with me for a little longer. I'd rather not explain anything right now. Just treat this as a spectacle. Act natural. Nothing here can hurt you." This was directed at Addie. "This won't take long. Just watch. All right?"

The Aldermen nodded. Addie held her objections.

"Let 'er go, Jake," Tretheway said.

The experiment lasted ten minutes. Just before the climax, Gum involuntarily shouted a warning, Addie's hand shot to her mouth and Ammerman tried to say something. When the metal ball smashed into the bottle, it shattered glass dramatically and sent fountains of milk into the air much higher than Tretheway had anticipated. Addie screamed. Gum jumped backwards in time to avoid the spray. Ammerman didn't. Jake quickly turned The Machine off. Tretheway, smiling, steadied the spent ball with his bare hand.

"Thank you, gentlemen, Addie," he said. "You've been more than patient. I think we can say the experiment was a success."

"Very, very impressive," Ammerman said.

"C'mon upstairs, Harold," Addie said, glaring at Tretheway. "I'll get that milk off your lapels before it dries."

"I still don't know what it is," Gum said.

"I'd rather not say any more just now," Tretheway said. "And I'd appreciate it if you kept this whole thing to yourselves. Just for a few days."

Gum looked hurt.

"Nobody else knows about this," Tretheway said.

"Nobody?" Gum brightened.

"Just me and Jake," Tretheway said. "And Doc Nooner."

"I guess there's no point in asking why the Doctor?"

Tretheway didn't answer.

"You know best," Gum said. He followed Addie and Ammerman up the stairs.

The next day, Tretheway was in Zulp's office. Backed by the professional opinion of Dr Nooner and the moral support of Jake, it took him the best part of the morning to swing Zulp over to their way of thinking. Zulp still didn't agree with them, but the slim possibility that the proposed experiment might work, might even prove him right, was too tempting. And he could offer no alternative.

"If it doesn't work, nobody's the loser," Tretheway said. Jake nodded behind him.

"True," Zulp said.

"And if it does work," Dr Nooner said, "it could prove you right."

"True also." Zulp rubbed one of his large ears. His brow creased. "Now let me get this straight. Proper planning. You want me to take Morgan out of jail. Take him to your house." He indicated Tretheway. "Let him take part in an experiment. Nothing dangerous." He looked at Dr Nooner. "And he might talk."

Nooner nodded.

Zulp plucked a pencil from the souvenir hollow coconut head on his desk and doodled a spiral on his blotter. "What the hell." He speared the pencil back into the coconut head. "Why not?" He looked at Tretheway. "When do you want him?"

"Tonight."

"Very well." Zulp sighed.

The afternoon was spent planning movements and security for that evening. Morgan had to be taken to The Machine because it had evolved into a device larger than Tretheway's cellar doors or windows and could not be easily moved. At one point, Zulp devised a plan that involved the RFY Light Infantry, but was talked out of it.

So, on the unusually cool, windy Friday evening of October 25, two beefy policemen escorted the hand-cuffed Alderman from the depressing Fort York Jail through the courtyard and into a waiting Black Maria. The driver locked the three men inside and climbed behind the wheel. He started the engine. As the rusting iron gates of the old prison squeaked open, two unmarked police cars took up their assigned positions—one ahead of the wagon, one behind—in a small procession. The uneventful three mile drive to the west end took about fifteen minutes.

When they reached Tretheway's street, the two police cars parked, one at each end of the crescent as specified in the plan, while the Black Maria backed up the driveway to its pre-determined spot. The driver unlocked the rear door. Tretheway appeared on the verandah. He watched as Morgan and his escorts crossed the lawn and mounted the verandah stairs.

"Hello, Morgan." Tretheway held the door open.

Morgan's reply was a simple smile.

Tretheway noticed the driver climbing back into the protected warmth of the Black Maria.

"Constable!" he shouted.

The policeman jumped from the running board and trotted toward Tretheway.

"That's your station, Constable." Tretheway pointed to the square of sidewalk where the officer was standing.

"Yes, sir."

"And keep your eyes open."

They took Alderman Morgan immediately to the cellar, removed his handcuffs and seated him in front of The Machine. Morgan did what he was told willingly. When he wasn't actually smiling, he just looked pleasant, a little vacant perhaps, but with no antagonism or belligerence. He had been like this, Dr Nooner told them, since the Michaelmas Day murder. No real problem—he washed himself, dressed himself and went to the bathroom without help, but when anyone spoke to him, his glazed eyes seemed to focus on a point about four feet behind the speaker. And still, he hadn't spoken.

The cellar was crowded, but not as much as it could have been; Tretheway's experiment had purposely not been advertised. Morgan of course was there, front and centre. Chief Zulp, Sergeant Wan Ho and Dr Nooner sat together on one bench which Jake had jury-rigged earlier. Alderman Gertrude Valentini and Controller MacCulla had been invited as the official representatives of City Council. Morgan's two police escorts blended into the background. And Addie stood on the cellar steps to ensure that her order that boarders not intrude was obeyed, and also to check the number of heads against the number of sandwiches she had made that afternoon. She had divided her time between that and cleaning the cellar. On such short notice, she could do little more than straighten the pile of cardboard boxes stored there by the students, wash and rehang the curtain that decorously hid a toilet (a legacy of the former owner standing embarrassingly beside the furnace), open the windows wide and sweep the coal dust back into the bin. At least, she thought, the atmosphere was fresher.

Polite chit-chat tapered off into apprehensive silence. The cellar, higher than average, was lit by one fixed billiard-type light directly above The Machine. Its large green reflector threw the strong light harshly downwards to give the setting a theatrical look.

While Jake's thin, sensitive fingers poked and prodded where Tretheway's couldn't, in some last minute adjustments, the gathering contemplated The Machine with suspicion. They seemed intimidated by its strange, alien appearance. Gertrude Valentini thought that the upper part of it resembled a gallows, while Wan Ho thought it looked more like a miniature ancient siege tower. Wan Ho was closer to the truth.

The five-foot-high wheeled tower stood on a horizontal platform thirty-six inches from the cellar floor at the head of a runway. The runway itself, which sloped toward the audience, was ten feet in length and twelve inches wide. A metal right-angled rod, four inches long, stuck out from the top of the tower. It was connected to a small electric motor. A four-and-a-half-foot length of fine but strong wire was fastened securely through a hole in the vertical portion of the metal rod. Hanging at the end of the wire, now stretched taut, was the focal point of The Machine—a five-pound chromium-plated lead ball approximately one and a half inches in diameter. Where the runway ended, at floor level, was another horizontal platform. It supported a clamping device. This was the business end.

After a whispered confirmation from Jake that all was set to go, Tretheway went to the front of The Machine and made an unnecessary announcement to the audience.

"If you'll give me your full attention, please."

He showed his profile to the group. "Jake, if you please."

Jake lifted a shapeless object, hidden beforehand, from the inside of the dustless ash sifter. He handed it to Tretheway. Under the light it became a royal blue velvet bag tied at the top with a gold, tasseled cord.

"Thank you," Tretheway said.

He slowly loosened the cord and carefully slid a bottle out of the bag. Jake took the bag away. Tretheway held the bottle at the very top and very bottom in his strong fingers. He moved it back and forth under the light to give the group, especially Morgan, a clear honest view in the same way a magician shows his theatre audience an empty sleeve or top hat. Every time the crystal decanter passed under the brilliant 300-watt light bulb, it sparkled like diamonds against the rich, liquid amber of its contents. It was a bottle of Seagram's Crown Royal twelve-year-old whiskey.

"Rye," Tretheway said. "Canadian rye whiskey. The best in the world."

All this time he watched Morgan intently. Once a flicker of interest seemed to appear in his eyes, a slight shifting of the hazy veil, but Tretheway couldn't be sure.

He handed the bottle reverently to Jake. "If you'd be so kind, Constable."

As Jake clamped the bottle firmly into position on the lower platform, he had the impression that Tretheway was greatly enjoying himself.

"The experiment is about to begin," Tretheway announced. "If you'd please hold your seats and your comments until it's over. Thank you." He stepped to the side of The Machine and nodded at Jake. "Constable."

Jake started the surprisingly quiet motor. The metal rod at the top of the tower twisted upward forty-five degrees, stopped at the horizontal, then twisted back ninety degrees through the vertical to horizontal again. It was obvious that this ninety-degree arc repeated and would go on repeating unless the motor stopped. The action was transmitted, jerkily at first, to the fine wire and then to the dangling metal ball. In a few short minutes, the action smoothed out so that the ball was swinging as rhythmically and predictably as a clock's pendulum. The startling whistling noise it made as it whirred through the air reached a crescendo each time it passed the lowest point—the point closest to the earth's centre.

Now Jake engaged a simple but ingenious set of gears behind The Machine that allowed gravity to pull the tower down the runway at a slow, inexorable rate of speed. Tretheway and Jake carefully backed away. The Machine was on its own.

For five minutes, everyone watched as the tower inched down the runway carrying the swinging missile closer and closer to the lower platform. Tretheway forced himself to watch Morgan instead of the hypnotic sphere. It became more and more obvious that, without interference, the whiskey bottle would soon meet destruction. At the eight-minute mark, when the tower was about three quarters of the way down, Tretheway noticed a change in Morgan. The glaze disappeared from his eyes. His limbs twitched almost imperceptibly. Life seemed to rekindle within him as the chromium ball swished back and forth through its arc, a single, brilliant highlight burning on its mirrored surface.

With less than a minute to go, Morgan switched his gaze from the ball to the bottle. Then he looked at Tretheway with a pleading expression. His mouth began to work. He returned his gaze helplessly to the bottle of whiskey.

On what everybody thought was the last swing, the ball only grazed the bottle enough to slightly change its trajectory and the compensatory return swing directed the ball's full force to the middle of the decanter. The crash was unbelievably loud.

Glass and contents once again scattered farther than Tretheway had anticipated. The thick, heady smell of expensive Canadian rye whiskey filled the cellar. Addie and Mrs Valentini screamed in unison. Jake leaped backwards about a foot. Dr Nooner and Mac both jumped to their feet. But most important of all, Alderman Morgan said his first words in almost a month.

"Bastarddammithell!" He jumped up. "Good whiskey! Deball the bugger who!" Morgan's eyes, vacant and dull for the last few weeks, were suddenly filled with lively indignation. He took a giant step toward The Machine, pointing with both hands at the wet floor. His legs buckled under him.

Dr Nooner, expecting a reaction of some sort, was beside him in seconds. Gertrude Valentini remained frozen, hands still covering her mouth as though a second scream might follow the first. It was Addie, Jake noticed, who arrived first at Morgan's elbow. She and Dr Nooner helped him to a comfortable old Morris chair that Tretheway occupied on cold winter mornings while he waited for the fire to draw. They sat him down. Mrs Valentini finally pushed in and jammed smelling salts under Morgan's nose. He shook his head in protest.

"That's enough," Dr Nooner instructed.

Morgan recovered quickly enough. He sat up by himself, smiled at those around him and seemed willing, if not eager, to talk. Tretheway watched him over Dr Nooner's shoulder. Morgan looked to him to be still in slight shock, still not quite sure what had happened and still, Tretheway thought, not aware of Alderman Taz's demise.

Wan Ho pushed in. "Dr Nooner, I wonder if . . ."

"Not yet, Sergeant," Dr Nooner said. "No questions for a few minutes."

"It's not that, Doc," Wan Ho said. "Could you look at the Chief?"

"Eh?"

"The Chief. Chief Zulp." Wan Ho went on. "He's still sitting there. He hasn't taken his eyes off that ball. Even after it hit the bottle."

"Oh?" Dr Nooner showed interest. He left Morgan with the two ladies and followed Wan Ho over to Zulp. Tretheway was close behind. Zulp was still sitting on the bench staring at the chromium-plated ball even though Jake had cut the motor immediately after the bottle disintegrated. Dr Nooner squatted down to Zulp's eye level. Zulp stared right through him.

"I'll be damned." Dr Nooner snapped his fingers in front of Zulp's eyes and smacked him lightly on both cheeks. Zulp didn't flinch. "C'mon, Chief. Snap out of it." Nooner smacked both cheeks again but much harder. "Wake up, Zulp!"

The Chief blinked several times and shook his head. His stare wandered for a moment aimlessly, focused on the Doctor, then over the Doctor's shoulder to Tretheway.

"Let's get on with it," Zulp ordered.

"It's over, Chief," Tretheway said.

"I still don't think it'll work," Zulp said. "What's over?"

"The experiment," Dr Nooner said.

"Morgan's talking again," Tretheway said.

"He is?" Zulp said. "I don't remember that. Where was I?" His brow wrinkled. "Must've nodded off. Tired lately. Pressure. This damn case."

"Anyway," Dr Nooner said, "Morgan's found his voice."

"Good. Good. Knew he would. Eventually. Bring him here for interrogation." Zulp looked suspiciously around the room. "There haven't been any questions asked yet. Have there?"

"No, no," Dr Nooner assured him. "But he needs a rest. As a matter of fact," Nooner stood up, "I think we all need a break." He caught Addie's eye.

"And some sandwiches," Addie helped out.

"And beer," Tretheway muttered, brightening.

For the next hour, the Tretheway household threw what for all the world appeared to be a party. The sun room comfortably held all the guests, even with the addition of O. Pitts and several other inquisitive boarders. Unusually mild air wafted through the open windows, spreading the heady fragrance of late fall flowers. Everyone, including Morgan, enjoyed assorted drinks, sandwiches and cigarettes while the music of Paul Whiteman spun from Addie's victrola. The babble of conversation skirted the reasons for the gathering.

Shortly after nine, Tretheway approached Dr Nooner. "Pretty soon, Doc?"

Dr Nooner examined his drink. "Yes." He put his glass down decisively. "Now. Morgan's been on vacation mentally for the last four weeks," he went on to explain. "He just got back tonight. He hasn't had time to absorb what's happened. Michaelmas Day. Lucifer Taz. Jail. The murder. And when he does . . ." Dr Nooner held his palms upward and shrugged. "Now," he repeated. "We'll question him now."

"Good." Tretheway started to leave.

"One more thing." Nooner stopped him. "This has to be done carefully."

Tretheway nodded.

"One person should ask all the questions."

"Zulp?" Tretheway questioned.

Nooner shook his head. He pointed at Tretheway. "You." He ticked off the points on his fingers. "One, he'll recognize you as a friend. Two, you're a police officer. And three, it's natural. This is your house. You're the host and he's comfortable here."

"All right with me," Tretheway said. "You'd better tell Zulp."

"Right." Dr Nooner made his way to Zulp's side and explained the situation. Zulp objected at first.

"Irregular. I should, really. Or even Wan Ho. However, expedient, I suppose. And I'll be right there," he agreed finally.

So it was Zulp, Morgan, Tretheway, Dr Nooner and Wan Ho who paraded out of the sun room, down the hall and into the parlour for questioning. The ladies excused themselves and Zulp had drawn the line at four against one despite Mac's protest.

"Police business," he said as he pulled the sliding parlour doors shut in front of Mac who had followed them down the hall. "Now let's get on with it." Zulp crossed the room and lowered himself into Tretheway's special chair.

Morgan sat on the uncomfortable love seat beside the electric fire. He cradled his fifth scotch carefully in both hands. Tretheway thought about sitting in a delicate reproduction of a Queen Anne chair but changed his mind and remained standing. Wan Ho sat on the settee across from the fire with his notebook out and ready. Dr Nooner sat beside him.

"Morgan," Tretheway began. "First of all, are you up to answering a few questions? How do you feel?"

"Top-hole. Tickety-boo," Morgan answered, a trifle too heartily.

"Fine," Tretheway said. "Let's go right back, then. To the beginning. Do you remember what you were doing a month ago? Twenty-eighth of September. Michaelmas Eve."

"We always had goose on Michaelmas."

"Eh?"

"When I was a boy. Goose for Michaelmas."

"Then you're familiar with that particular holiday?"

"Certainly. Mind you, I haven't thought about it for years." Morgan frowned as though trying to remember something. "Until now."

"Michaelmas was on Sunday. Do you remember what you were doing the day before? Saturday?"

"Saturday," Morgan repeated. "Yes. I do. A bond drive dinner at the armouries." He pointed to Zulp. "You were there. Big piss-up afterwards."

"That's right," Zulp explained. "I was there. Just for the dinner."

"Go on, Morgan," Tretheway said.

"We stayed for the dance."

"Who's we?" Tretheway asked.

"Oh, just about everybody. The Mayor. Pennylegion. Mac-Culla. O'Dell. Just about all the Council.

"Taz? Lucifer Taz?"

"Yes." Morgan frowned again. "He was there."

"When did you leave?"

"Not right away. We stayed pretty late. Lived it up. Spun the ladies around the floor. Had a fair amount to drink."

Tretheway said nothing while Morgan ferreted out pictures filed away in his memory a month before.

"I remember now," he said. "We . . . Lucifer and I drove to the University. In his car."

"Why the University?" Tretheway asked.

"He wouldn't say. Said it was a secret. Secret meeting. We laughed a lot at this time. We were both pretty potted."

"Did you go in the University?"

"Not at first. I sat in the car. Lucifer parked a good two furlongs from the building. He got out and told me to wait. Then he walked away. Toward the University."

"And you never saw him again . . ." Tretheway bit his tongue.

"What?" Morgan glanced around the room as though looking for someone. "No. That's not right."

"Look, Morgan," Tretheway said. "Just sit back and finish your story. As much as you can remember. Take your time. I won't interrupt you anymore."

"If that's what you want," Morgan said.

Tretheway nodded.

"Well, I sat there for a while. I don't know how long. Then I followed Lucifer. Or tried." His teeth made indentations on his lower lip as he struggled to piece events together. "I remember walking across the soccer field. The grass was wet. Raining. Over the cinder track. I scratched myself on some bushes. Then the main building. The rear of University Hall. A light. There was a flickering light. Like fire. Through the stained glass window. The one with the Devil. Lucifer. Isn't that odd? And there was organ music. Wagner. Walked around the front. Open. Went up the stairs." Morgan gulped half his drink. Part of him now trying desperately not to remember. "I went into the chapel. Lucifer was there. I told you I saw him again. Alone. Sitting in a chair. Something was burning. And there were flowers. I went to him. He had this . . . this sword . . . Oh God . . ."

"Easy, Morgan," Dr Nooner said quietly.

"I grabbed the handle." Morgan's temples were glistening. His eyes were far too large. He dropped his glass in his lap. "I pulled it out of Lucifer. He's not here, is he? He fell down. Rolled over. His eyes were . . . he's gone, isn't he? He's . . ." Morgan stood up suddenly. His glass shattered on the hardwood floor.

"That's enough, Morgan." Tretheway went to Morgan and steadied him gently. "Sit down. It's all over."

For the next few minutes, the only sound in the parlour was Morgan's polite sobbing.

The party, or gathering, ended shortly after. At Dr Nooner's insistence, Morgan was taken to the hospital instead of jail. At Zulp's insistence, he was still under heavy guard.

Tretheway tried to bring up Hallowe'en, but Zulp put him off until Monday.

"But Hallowe'en's Thursday," Tretheway protested.

"I said Monday, dammit. In my office."

On Monday morning, first thing, it was obvious that Zulp's original opinion about the Michaelmas murder had not only held firm, but hardened into concrete.

"Cock-and-bull story!" Zulp said.

Tretheway and Wan Ho were his captive audience. Jake waited in the hall outside Zulp's office.

"We're proceeding with the case," Zulp said. "The charge stands."

"Do you think Alderman Morgan was lying?" Tretheway asked.

"I don't think he knows. I mean, all that booze. Not talking for a month. Shock. He went funny. Never-never land."

"What about the footprints behind the chapel?" Wan Ho asked.

"Students," Zulp countered. "Proves nothing. Doesn't change the other facts. Does it?"

Tretheway and Wan Ho sat without answering.

"Morgan's still placed at the scene. At the right time. Holding the sword. Did he see anybody else? Did anybody see anybody else? Tell me I'm wrong."

"What about the music?" Tretheway asked.

"From a student residence."

"Wagner?" Wan Ho asked.

"Why not? I like him."

"But why did Morgan do it?" Tretheway asked. "Where's the motive?"

"It'll turn up," Zulp said confidently. He stood up, his usual signal for an end to discussion.

Wan Ho stood up. Tretheway didn't.

"One more thing, Chief, if you please," Tretheway said.

"Make it short," Zulp snapped.

"What are you going to do about Hallowe'en?"

The wrinkles on Zulp's face seemed even deeper when he flushed. "Inspector Tretheway," he said with control. "I don't know what you are going to do about Hallowe'en, but I will be at home, with Mrs Zulp, handing out bags of candy."

"Oh," Tretheway said.

"On second thought." Zulp smiled. "I do know what you are going to do. Or, at least, I know what you are not going to do." His smile disappeared. "You're not going to play Boston Blackie. Or Sherlock Holmes. You're not going to call the dispatcher. Or organize chases. Is that clear?"

"Yes, Sir." Tretheway stood up.

"Now." Zulp smoothed the front of his tunic. "Take my advice. Spend a quiet evening at home. Hand out treats. Read. Play cards. Listen to the radio. And control yourself."

Tretheway and Wan Ho stood motionless.

"That's all." Zulp dismissed them.

They turned smartly and left the office. Outside, Jake fell into step beside Tretheway. He knew better than to ask anything. Besides, he had heard the louder parts of the discussion through the thick oak door.

On All Hallow's Eve, the weather changed as though to match the mood of the holiday. The temperature dropped close to the freezing mark and a capricious, blustery wind ushered a cold front across the southern part of the province. When the clouds covered the full moon, cold darts of rain lanced into squealing groups of scurrying, costumed children running from house to house, clutching pillow cases or brown paper bags brimming with treats. And when the clouds scudded on, the moon threw shimmering, mysterious shadows of black cats, witches, spiders, bats, and most scary of all, unknown things, on the variegated greys of wet sidewalks and lawns. To the young, it was a delicious, giggly fear. But to others . . .

By eight o'clock, Addie had handed out fifty-seven prepared bags of goodies to assorted ghosts, pirates, tramps, ballet dancers, clowns, fairy princesses, one ugly toad, four tin men, (*The Wizard of Oz* had played at the local cinema two weeks before) and other creatures too amorphous to classify.

The children ranged from pre-schoolers, chaperoned by their parents, to sixth-graders. As the evening progressed, the stream of trick-or-treaters lessened in number but grew in years. By nine-thirty, it had slowed to a trickle of ten year olds, mostly ghosts. And the last group was four first-year high school boys, with hasty daubs of lipstick and smears of eyebrow pencil on their faces as a weak excuse for a costume. They left the Tretheways', pushing and jostling each other off the sidewalk, at ten o'clock.

"Eighty-three children," Addie said. She was busy tidying up the card table they had set up in the front hall for Hallowe'en. "A dozen more than last year." The number of callers the Tretheways had was well above average. Reputations travel and Addie packed a mean Hallowe'en bag. "That leaves seventeen for your lunches."

Tretheway made a face behind Addie's back.

"That's great, Addie," Jake said.

Tretheway and Jake were sitting in the parlour with the sliding doors open close to the front entrance, ostensibly to help Addie hand out treats, but also to be near the hall phone. They had all avoided the obvious topic until now.

"It's after ten," Addie said. She was carrying the left-over bags of candy back to the kitchen. "It looks like it might be a quiet Hallowe'en." Her voice rose questioningly as she walked past the parlour.

"Could be, Addie," Jake answered.

Tretheway remained silent.

Addie continued down the hall. Tretheway and Jake listened while cupboard doors banged noisily in the kitchen for five minutes before she went into the sun room to look for company.

"It has been pretty quiet," Jake said.

"You're right," Tretheway said.

"Do you think it will stay quiet?"

"I hope so. But don't get into your pajamas yet."

Except for trips to the ice box for Molson Blue, the two men sat in the parlour half-listening to the "Kraft Music Hall." Tretheway didn't care at all for Bing Crosby, but waited for the parts of the program when Bob Burns performed. Jake did exactly the opposite. At eleven o'clock, while Jake fiddled with the dial to get the local news and Tretheway rested low in his special chair, the phone rang. Addie easily got there first. Tretheway and Jake waited.

Addie appeared in the opening of the parlour doors. She was pale. Optimism had disappeared from her face.

"That was Mrs Ammerman. She can't find Harold."

Jake was first at Addie's side.

"Sit here, Addie." Tretheway pushed himself to the front of his chair. By the time he was standing up, Jake had made Addie comfortable on the settee.

"Try not to worry, Addie," Jake said.

"Do you think . . ." Addie started.

"Don't try and guess," Tretheway said. "You know Ammerman. He's absent-minded. Probably made a wrong turn somewhere."

"I don't know," Addie said.

"What did Mrs Ammerman say?" Tretheway asked.

"That Harold left the house just after supper. He'd gone to the Children's Garden. The clubhouse. To help out at the party. The costume judging. But she said that was over at nine. He never came home." Addie looked up at Tretheway. "Where could he be?"

"We'll find out." Tretheway caught Jake's eye. "Get the car."

Jake hurried out of the room.

"Put the kettle on, Addie." Tretheway drained the beer bottle beside his chair. "We won't be long."

Jake backed jerkily down the driveway. The Pontiac protested the cold start by coughing, sputtering and finally stalling. "Damn!" He pulled the choke out farther and restarted the engine as Tretheway climbed into the passenger seat.

"Let's go, Jake," Tretheway ordered.

"Where?" Jake asked.

"You know where Ammerman lives?"

"Not far from the park."

"Go there."

Jake flicked the high beams on as they pulled into the dark street and headed toward the park. He started the wipers.

"No," Tretheway said to the windshield.

"Eh?" Jake said.

"Gum."

"What?"

"Gum. Bartholomew Gum. Doesn't he work with Ammerman on this Hallowe'en thing?"

"Ah . . . yes."

"Do you know where he lives?"

"Right across from the park."

"Go there."

In less than five minutes, Jake turned the heavy convertible into Bartholomew Gum's narrow driveway. Seconds later, they stood on Gum's front lawn, pulling their police-issue rubber capes around them against the weather and staring up at a light in the attic window.

"Is that Gum's room?" Tretheway asked.

"I think so."

"Let's check the garage."

The gravel crunched beneath their feet. Through the small, dusty window of the garage, they saw Gum's bicycle, locked and leaning against his mother's '28 Essex.

"He's home," Jake said.

"I'm surprised he's up this late," Tretheway added.

They walked back around to the front door.

"We'll just have to knock until he hears us," Tretheway said.

"And wake his mother?"

"Can't be helped." Tretheway knocked on the door. The wind whipped the sound harmlessly away. Tretheway knocked again, or hammered really, much harder, while Jake stood on the lawn watching the third floor window. He noticed a movement. The window opened.

"Go away!" Bartholomew Gum shouted. "No more candy!" The window started to close.

"Gum!" Jake shouted as quietly as he could. "Bartholomew Gum! It's me! Jake!"

The window opened again. Bartholomew Gum leaned out and stared down at the voice.

"C'mon down," Jake shouted. "It's important!"

"It's after eleven!" Gum shouted back.

Tretheway loomed into Gum's view. "Get the hell down here!" The window closed.

Tretheway and Jake scurried back to the protection of the verandah. When Gum finally appeared, he had heavy rubber boots on and a Scouter's trench coat over his pajamas. He closed the front door quietly behind him.

"I hope we didn't wake your mother," Jake said.

"She sleeps on her good ear," Gum answered. "What's going on?"

"Ammerman's missing," Tretheway said.

"Harold?" Gum looked surprised. "I was with him earlier."

"When earlier?" Tretheway asked.

"Oh, nine o'clock. Maybe even before that. We judged the kids pretty fast because of the weather."

"Where, Bartholomew?" Jake asked.

"The Children's Garden. In the clubhouse." Gum thought for a moment. "Harold was there when I left. Cleaning up." He pointed across the street to the dim outline of the clubhouse, partially obscured by the trees in the park. "As a matter of fact, I think there's still a light on over there."

"Is there a phone?"

"No. It's just a roughed-in workroom, really. And a storage area."

"You have your flashlight, Jake?"

Jake patted his pocket and nodded.

"Let's take a look," Tretheway said.

They crossed the street, three shadows huddled together.

The moon shone through a hole in the clouds to show them a pathway through the maze of oddly shaped, exotic trees. Tretheway, Jake and Gum dodged around Scheidecker Crabs, Weeping Nootkas, Crimson King Norway Maples, Hinoki Fals Cypresses and other angular Oriental specimens. All had been neatly labelled—unpronounceable Latin names engraved on metal tags and attached to the proper trees—by the Fort York Royal Botanical Garden Society.

Tretheway, leading the way, reached the actual garden first. About an acre in size, it was bordered on three sides by a six-foot cedar hedge. The low, ivy-covered clubhouse, topped by a louvered cupola with an ornate weathervane, edged the fourth side. By this time of year, only four or five large pumpkins had escaped the children's harvest. A few late annuals still bloomed, but these would go with the first frost—maybe tonight.

The moon ducked behind a cloud. Tretheway bumped into something solid.

"Damn!" He stepped back. "What the hell's that?"

A sturdy post set into the ground supported an old suit of clothes stuffed with straw. Its arms, a two-by-two wooden cross-piece, stood out perpendicularly from the body. Old cowboy gauntlets were sewn on the cuffs for hands. In deference to the war, a dishpan-like steel helmet was strapped onto the ball of straw that served as a head.

"It's the scarecrow," Gum said unnecessarily. "I don't know if it works, but the kids enjoy it."

Tretheway rubbed his forehead. "Well, watch out for it." He continued to the clubhouse. Jake and Gum followed. Tretheway tried the door.

"It's not locked." Tretheway barged in, too carelessly, Jake thought. Jake entered warily, but Gum hung back.

"Ammerman!" Tretheway shouted. "You in here?"

There was no answer. The interior of the workroom smelled of damp earth. A single light bulb hanging from the ceiling glowed weakly. Most of the floor space was taken up with long potting tables covered with small hand tools, plant containers, a hot plate, a dented kettle, an old mantel radio, variously sized tuberous roots and boxes of planting records. One wall was covered with botanical charts. Another held a rack for the storage of long tools such as rakes, hoes, cultivators, shovels and pruning shears. There were bushel baskets stacked in two corners.

"C'mon in, Bartholomew," Jake said. "Ammerman's not here."

Gum came in slowly, looking around. "He was here. Did you check everywhere?"

Tretheway poked his head into the storage area. He turned back. "Nothing there." A reflection caught his eye. "What's that?"

"Where?" Jake said.

"There." Tretheway pointed to the floor.

Jake picked up a shiny metallic object about three inches long and pointed at one end.

"Looks like . . . an arrowhead. Or spear tip." Jake handed it to Tretheway. He turned it around in his thick fingers and examined the end that wasn't pointed.

"Clean break," Tretheway said. "It broke away from something. Looks important, doesn't it?"

Jake nodded. "Part of a costume?"

"It's no garden tool." Tretheway looked at Gum. "Do you remember anything like this?"

"Not offhand," Gum said. "There were some Indians. But they had little arrows. An African native. He had a spear. Could've been him."

Tretheway nodded. "Anything else?"

Gum thought for a moment and then snapped his fingers. "A Roman soldier! I'll bet that's it. I know the kid, too."

"Could you find out for sure?" Tretheway asked.

"Sure," Gum said.

"Is it important?" Jake asked.

"Probably not." Tretheway pushed his hand under his cape and stuffed the alleged spearhead into his pocket. "Just something else to file."

"And we still haven't found Ammerman," Jake said.

"Where can we look now?" Gum asked.

"The woods," Tretheway said.

"The woods?" Gum repeated.

"At night?" Jake said.

"If Ammerman did make a wrong turn, an absent-minded mistake, he's still wandering around out there." Tretheway flung his arm in the direction of the street. "Somewhere. In no danger. If someone wanted to hurt him, they'd do it here. Which they haven't. Or they'd take him away." He flung his arm in the opposite direction. "Down the woods."

"Could we wait until morning?" Gum said.

"We could call for help," Jake suggested.

"What's the time?" Tretheway snapped.

"Eleven-twenty," Jake said.

"We have forty minutes." Tretheway went to the tool rack and picked up a long-handled shovel. "Gentlemen, choose your weapons."

They decided by a two-to-one vote to stick together. Tretheway, not usually given to democratic procedure, went along in this case because of the short time left and because half of his force was civilian. Besides, he reasoned, if they split up, they might attack each other in the darkness. Tretheway marched at the head of the procession brandishing his garden shovel. Jake was next, a wicked three-pronged cultivator held across his chest like a hockey stick in the cross-check position; Gum, a little slower and slightly behind, guarded the rear. Gum had chosen a lawn rake for his defense or attack. At one point when they closed up and crossed a rise in the ground, with the moon a white, shimmering globe behind them, they looked as though they had been cut out of black construction paper and pasted on a third grade classroom window for the holiday.

Tretheway struck west immediately. Grass gave way to dirt at the top of the first trail.

"I thought you guys carried guns," Gum said to the backs of the other two.

"Mine's at the office," Jake said.

"Keep it down," Tretheway ordered.

Coote's Paradise was kept as close as possible to nature with very little housekeeping. Dead trees rotted where they fell. Leaves, at this time of year, covered the floor of the ravine and creeks ran without the aid of concrete spillways or dams. The only obvious marks of civilization, other than the discreetly placed, camouflaged litter barrels, were the trail markers. Neat, dark-stained posts and matching crosspieces, branded with the names of the trails, marked the way for neophyte hikers. They were unnecessary for Tretheway. He was familiar with the woods because of his Sunday walks. Jake and Gum, of course, had roamed the ravine as children before there was any need for signposts or litter barrels.

They entered the woods and slipped out of sight down Caleb's Walk. By alternately jogging and walking, or keeping what Gum called Scout's pace, they were able to cover an amazing amount of ground. The trail crossed Westdale Brook, then forked left to the University grounds. From there, they followed yet another trail called Pinery, back into the woods to the edge of the marsh, then along a tortuous, up-and-down path labelled Arnott's Walk. Tretheway stopped. Jake and Gum stopped also and tried to see around Tretheway. From behind a larger than usual hump in the trail ahead, they heard quiet voices and saw a reflection of flickering light.

"What's over the hill?" Tretheway whispered.

"Kingfisher Point," Jake whispered back nervously.

"It's a landing," Gum whispered, as nervously as Jake.

"When I say go, yell like hell and follow me over the hill," Tretheway said.

"Eh?" Gum said.

"But what if . . ." Jake started.

"Go!" Tretheway charged over the rise. His yell scared Jake and Gum but they followed. Their charge had a predictable effect on the four FYU first year students, two boys, two girls, enjoying a private party around a warming fire. They had also been drinking dark Jamaican rum to ward off the cold, which exaggerated the improbable sight made by Tretheway's group.

Both girls screamed immediately. The four of them jumped to their feet, and after a frozen second, turned and ran. Tretheway realized almost at once that these unfortunates were not the quarry. He stopped in his tracks. Jake and Gum bumped behind him. Before Tretheway could do anything, the student quartet had climbed back up the ravine—not on a trail but through the trees—and could be followed easily for the next five minutes by the sounds of crashing underbrush.

"Damn!" Tretheway said.

"Maybe we should follow them and explain," Jake said.

"They looked awfully scared," Gum said.

"Take too long," Tretheway replied. "They shouldn't've been here anyway."

"My God." A smile showed through Jake's words. "I wonder what they thought?"

Tretheway chuckled.

"I wonder what they'll tell their friends?" Gum said.

They mused on and imagined the start of a legend about ghostly gardeners that would be handed down over the years.

"Shouldn't we be moving on?" Jake finally suggested.

"I suppose so," Tretheway said. "But we've probably scared off anybody within miles. Let's go."

They took the South Shore Trail to Sassafras Point, checked Cockpit Island, doubled back to Ginger Valley and Princess Point, all without success.

"Let's check the road," Tretheway said.

They followed the Ravine Road all the way back to where it joined Caleb's Walk. Tretheway took a huge handkerchief from his pocket and wiped the rain from his face.

"Where to now?" Gum asked.

"What's the time?" Tretheway said.

"Twelve-ten," Jake said.

Tretheway sighed. "Might as well go home." He led the way back over Caleb's Walk. Their pace was much slower than it had been fifty minutes before. By the time they left the woods proper, the rain had stopped and the moon showed itself once again.

"Looks like it might clear," Gum said.

Neither Tretheway nor Jake answered. The wind still blew cold as they passed the Children's Garden on their way to Gum's house.

Tretheway stopped. "Jake." He sniffed the air.

"Hm?"

"What's that smell?"

Jake raised his head and imitated Tretheway. Gum joined in to further test the air.

"Sassafras," they said together.

"Around here?" Tretheway said.

"No," Jake said. "At least a mile away."

"Sassafras Point," Gum confirmed.

"It's coming from over there." Tretheway looked at the clubhouse suspiciously. "Look at the scarecrow."

"What about it?" Jake stopped beside Tretheway.

The scarecrow was plainly visible, silhouetted against the moon-white stucco of the clubhouse.

"Doesn't it look different?" Tretheway said.

The three of them stared intently across the dark grey field.

"How?" Gum asked.

"The head," Tretheway said.

"The helmet's gone," Jake said.

"And it looks . . . bigger," Gum said.

"Gimme your light," Tretheway said.

They approached the scarecrow cautiously. Tretheway kicked something.

"What's that?" He shone the flashlight on the ground.

"It's the scarecrow," Jake said. "At least, the old one."

"Then what . . ." Gum started.

The flashlight's beam travelled over the ground the few remaining feet to the post. Several loose sassafras leaves lay crushed around its base. Then, steady in Tretheway's hand, the revealing light rose upwards to show a figure, presumably a man's, tied grotesquely to the post in the same position as the old scarecrow. He was dressed in a baggy tweed suit and sodden trench coat. A small sassafras branch was caught in the coat's buckle. Where his ball of hay, or head, should be, was a large Hallowe'en pumpkin.

"That's the pumpkin we had for the kids," Gum said.

Tretheway shone the flashlight into the triangular eyeholes of the large Jack-O-Lantern. The wide-open, glassy eyes of Harold

Ammerman reflected the beam as spectacularly as a cat's eyes reflect the headlights of a passing car.

"Jezuz." Tretheway flicked off the light.

The moon returned to the privacy of the clouds. It started to spit rain again.

NOVEMBER

Alderman Harold Ammerman was buried on Friday, November 1, before the sun went down, according to Jewish custom. Dr Nooner had discovered in a hurried but efficient medical examination that the cause of death was heart failure. And the horrified facial expression, plus the macabre situation in which Ammerman was discovered, forced all those involved, including Zulp, to agree upon one conclusion. Simply, Harold Ammerman had been scared to death.

On other theories, however, there were divergent thoughts.

"The sassafras leaves," Zulp said. "They're the key."

"Eh?" Tretheway blinked. Wan Ho was also taken aback. So were Jake and Gum, who were sitting beside each other near the door. It was Monday and they had all been called into Zulp's office for an impromptu review of the latest murder; Wan Ho in his official capacity and the others because they had found the body. "You're just too much involved," Zulp had said to Tretheway. "You're always . . . ah . . . there." Zulp had been shocked at Ammerman's death but also angry at Tretheway for once again being first on the scene. He had softened his stand somewhat when he had learned that Tretheway had been dragged by Mrs Ammerman into the discovery of yet another body.

Over the weekend, the investigation had run into its customary cul-de-sac. It seemed that Hallowe'en *was* the perfect night for a murder. Everyone is in disguise; beings sneak about in the darkness with impunity; the bizarre becomes the norm, and strange, inexplicable things traditionally happen. There were no official suspects. Theories, on the other hand, were not scarce.

"It's an aphrodisiac, you know," Zulp continued.

"Eh?" Tretheway repeated.

"You boil it up. Brew it. Preferably over an open fire. At night. Then give it to someone you want to . . . you know."

"That's sassafras tea," Gum said. "My mother drinks sassafras tea."

116

"That's none of our business, Gum," Zulp said.

"But it's a medicine," Gum protested.

"Like a tonic, I thought," Tretheway said.

"That's right," Jake confirmed. "It's medicinal. Also used in the manufacture of cosmetics, I think."

"Root beer, too," Wan Ho offered. "You make it with the roots."

"I didn't know that," Jake said.

"We have here an affaire d'amour!" Zulp shouted to regain the group's lost attention. He succeeded. No one answered.

"A tryst," Zulp whispered. "A secret rendezvous."

"Sir." Wan Ho recovered first. "I don't understand."

Tretheway looked over his shoulder and saw by the expressions on Jake's and Gum's faces that they didn't understand either. He turned back to Zulp. "I'm lost too, Sir."

Zulp entwined his pudgy fingers over his chest just below his WWI ribbons, and stared at the ceiling. A full minute passed. Tretheway and Wan Ho both glanced upward in search of a possible clue.

"Alderman Ammerman was brewing, or going to brew sassafras tea," Zulp began, "for a lady friend. He was alone. Children gone home. Dark rainy night. Cozy clubhouse. Probably candles. Maybe some music. Sandwiches. Harold readying the feast with a twinkle in his eye."

"But we didn't see him," Tretheway said.

"He didn't want you to see him. Hid somewhere." Zulp smiled. "Probably watched you three go on your dumb hike."

"But . . ."

"Let me finish the picture for you, Tretheway. The other woman didn't turn up. But her husband did. Confrontation. J'accuse! Ammerman protests. A tussle. More shouting. A final struggle. Ammerman clutches his chest." Zulp made a noise like a child gargling. "The husband silences forever the invader of his wife's honour."

"Ammerman?" Tretheway said.

"Still waters."

"He's over seventy," Gum protested.

"Never too old."

"But who?" Wan Ho said.

"Dammit, Sergeant. I can't do everything. Do a little digging. Leg work. This man's dangerous."

A thoughtful silence followed Zulp's conjecture. Tretheway waited.

"You know what I think?" he asked finally.

"Tretheway," Zulp interrupted. "Remember one thing. You're here because you're a witness. Along with those other two." He pointed over Tretheway's head at Jake and Gum. "You're not here in an official capacity."

"It wouldn't hurt to hear any suggestions," Wan Ho said.

"Well," Zulp said.

"I need all the help I can get," Wan Ho persisted.

"I suppose. Open mind and all that."

"To start with," Tretheway jumped in. "I think the sassafras leaves show only one thing. That they—I mean Ammerman and captors—had been to Sassafras Point. Nothing more." Tretheway stood up bringing the chair with him. He pushed it off his buttocks. "What makes me mad is that I think they were down the woods at the same time we were." He indicated Jake and Gum. "Sheer dumb luck we didn't see them. Probably crossed trails. But anyway, they probably ran old Harold around the woods. Up and down the hills. That'd be pretty gruelling for a man his age. Poor old bugger." Tretheway put his hands behind his back. He stared out the window. A light snow was falling. "It was murder."

"And you still keep referring to 'they'. Plural," Wan Ho said.

"That's right," Tretheway said. "I'd say there were at least two. Maybe more."

Zulp's eyebrows rose at the mention of more than two, but for the first time in the case, he didn't argue against the possibility. It didn't, however, help his mood.

"Then who the hell was it?" he said to Tretheway.

"I don't know." Tretheway squeezed back into the chair.

"Do you know?" Zulp asked Wan Ho.

Wan Ho shook his head.

"Then we're right back where we started." Zulp sat down heavily.

"Except for your theory," Tretheway said.

"Eh?"

"The love triangle. It's worth investigating."

"Yes. Of course." Zulp coughed self-consciously. He checked his watch. "That's a good point to finish on. You two anything to add?" He looked across the room at Jake and Gum. They both shook their heads.

"We should really release Morgan," Wan Ho said.

"I suppose," Zulp agreed. He jumped up. "That's it, then. Routine police work. Hop to it."

"Ah . . ." Tretheway ventured. "There's one more thing."

"What now?" Zulp said.

Everyone looked at Tretheway.

"What about this month?" He looked at Zulp. "Just in case your theory doesn't . . . work out. Then I think something will happen in November."

"Wouldn't hurt to have a back-up plan," Wan Ho said. "Just in case."

"Oh, I don't know." Zulp sighed and sat down again. He was beginning to feel like a yo-yo.

"Have you picked a holiday?" Wan Ho asked.

Now Tretheway sighed. It seemed that even the traffic outside had stopped moving to hear his answer.

"November 11."

"What?" Zulp said. The traffic noise picked up.

"Armistice Day."

Zulp jumped up and leaned across his desk. Tretheway felt obligated to do the same, except for leaning across the desk. Zulp was three inches short of rubbing eyeballs with Tretheway. "Do you know something I don't know? You know I don't like surprises. Or secrets."

"Nothing really," Tretheway said, not backing off. "It's another educated guess."

Before he could help himself, Zulp sat down again. "Please explain."

"Nothing to explain," Tretheway started. "Armistice Day is one week from today. Monday. I'm not sure how it'll happen. Probably something warlike. Gun. Hand grenade. Bayonet. Something fitting the occasion. And probably at the eleventh hour." Tretheway felt for a cigar, then remembered where he was. "You know, it would really be fitting, for the murderer, I mean, if it happened at the Cenotaph."

"At eleven o'clock?" Zulp asked. "During the service?"

"There'll be hundreds of people there," Wan Ho said.

"I know," Tretheway answered. "But there's been a boldness to all of the murders. And the other things. They've always taken a chance. An unnecessary one. Where they could've been caught."

"You think it's part of their procedure? Or maybe for a thrill?" Wan Ho said.

"Or a philosophy of some sort," Tretheway said.

"I still say it's too risky for the murderer," Zulp said. "I mean, right downtown. All those witnesses."

"You're probably right," Tretheway agreed. "But for safety's sake . . ."

"All right. All right," Zulp said. "Extra men. Flying Squads, all that. I suppose you know who."

"Pardon?" Tretheway said.

"Who's going to be shot. Or blown up. Or whatever."

"It should be someone associated with the military." Tretheway looked around the room. "Any suggestions?"

"Morgan Morgan was in the first World War," Jake said.

"The Mayor was a fireman," Wan Ho offered.

Tretheway looked at Zulp. "Anybody else?" He fished for an answer he knew already. "Isn't there anyone on Council you consider more military than anyone else?"

"Not really," Zulp said. "These days everyone has some . . ." He slammed his palm on the desk top. "Wakeley! Major-General F. McKnight Wakeley!"

"That's right," Wan Ho said. "Always saluting. Spit and polish. Wears a uniform more than a regular."

"He marches, never walks," Jake added. "Perfect."

"He'd be my choice," Tretheway said.

"Now we're getting somewhere," Zulp said. "We should be making plans. Maybe alert the army. They'll be here anyway."

"It's still conjecture," Tretheway warned.

"Can't take a chance," Zulp said.

"I agree," Tretheway went on. "But I think here, safety lies in discretion. In silence. No one outside this room should know about this."

A conspiracy appealed to Zulp as much as a flamboyant, complicated plan. "That's true," he said. "Mum's the word." His eyes flitted from face to face, coming to rest finally on the only civilian. "You got that, Gum?"

Gum nodded hastily.

"I have a couple of key men that should be told," Wan Ho said. "They can be trusted."

"You know best," Tretheway said.

"You don't think we should tell the Council members?" Zulp stood up. He hoped the meeting was over.

"No," Tretheway said. "Especially the Council members."

"Forewarned is forearmed," Wan Ho said.

"That's a two-edged sword," Tretheway said.

"Cheaters never prosper," Gum said.

Everyone stared at Gum.

During the next week only two pertinent events came to light. The first had to do with the young trick-or-treater who masqueraded as a Roman soldier. On investigation, his spear turned out to be an elaborate curtain rod since returned to its proper place in his mother's living room. It was intact.

The second discovery was due more to luck than good police work. It was mid-week, early morning. Tretheway and Jake were driving Alderman Gum to the City Hall on their way to Central. They were discussing the case in general.

"And to think I used to like holidays," Gum groaned. "It's been a bad year, so far."

"Except for January," Jake said.

"Well . . . even then," Gum said.

"Eh?" Tretheway started.

"Nothing special, really," Gum said. "And it happened just to me."

"On a holiday?" Tretheway asked.

"The first."

"New Year's Day?" Tretheway's scalp went pins and needles. "You'd better tell me the whole thing. What happened? Where were you?"

"At your place," Gum began.

"It happened there?" Tretheway asked.

"No, no. I was at your New Year's Eve party first. The one you always have. The whole Council was there. It was when I got home that it happened."

Tretheway nodded. "Go on."

"Well, by the time I got home and fell asleep," Gum went on, "it must've been two o'clock in the morning. Something woke me. Sounded like footsteps. Downstairs. I thought it was Mother at first. But then I heard more than one set. I jumped right out of bed and ran downstairs. I guess I made plenty of noise myself. Bumped into walls. Knocked a lamp over. I was half asleep. Anyway, when I got downstairs, no one was there. I think I heard footsteps again. Running. And a door close. But I can't be sure."

"Why the hell didn't you call the police?" Tretheway said.

"Why? I never did see anything. Even outside. By the time I woke up completely, I thought maybe I'd dreamt the whole thing."

"What about the door?" Tretheway asked.

"It was unlocked, but shut. No marks on it. I could've left it like that myself."

"Then you think now that it was a dream?" Tretheway asked.

"There was one thing I couldn't figure."

"What's that?"

"A lump of coal."

"Eh?"

"Coal. A piece about as big as your fist. Just sitting on the table in the front hall."

Tretheway stood up and walked around behind the chesterfield. "That rounds it out." He clenched his hands behind his back as best he could. "I always wondered why it started in February."

"What do you mean?" Gum asked. Jake, too, looked to Tretheway for an answer.

"What nationality are you?" Tretheway asked Gum.

"Pardon?"

"Where are you from? What country?"

"Canada."

"And your parents?"

"The same."

"Ever heard of first footing?" Tretheway asked.

Gum shook his head.

"Neither have I," Jake said.

Tretheway shrugged his huge shoulders. "Colonists," he muttered.

Near the end of the week, Tretheway thought it appropriate to check on the whereabouts and general well-being of Alderman

F. McKnight Wakeley. When contacted by phone, however, Wakeley's housekeeper told Tretheway that he was on manoeuvres with his Cadet Corps unit.

"Will he be back in time for the Armistice Day program?" Tretheway asked her.

"Oh, he'd rather die than miss that," she said.

Tretheway winced at her choice of words.

On Sunday MacCulla arrived at the Tretheways' to participate in the weekly tramp through the woods. Before they left, Tretheway and Jake had a brief discussion of last minute details about the special preparations for Armistice Day. Fred, the Labrador, also went with them. O. Pitts decided to go at the last minute.

It was sunny, but bracing. The two inches of snow that had fallen earlier showed the busy, frantic tracks of small animals. Once in the woods, there was little conversation, except for O. Pitts. Tretheway, muffled against the fifteen-knot wind, ignored Pitts the several times he tried to bring up the murders. Jake remained polite but didn't encourage him. And MacCulla showed no interest at all.

Sunday's weather held through Monday. The sun sparkled shamelessly in the clear atmosphere and the snow crunched coldly under the feet of the many celebrants now gathered around the Cenotaph. Flags snapping noisily in the breeze provided the only colour against the sombre background of civilian mourning dress and wartime uniforms.

The largest contingent, by far, was the RFYLI. As well as full battalion of regular foot soldiers, they supplied a reserve unit, a platoon of WWI veterans, a colour party and a section of duty buglers. The Navy and Air Force were also well represented. Cadets from all three services, each affiliated with an active unit, had marched in the parade with the men they might one day replace. And the ever-present Scouts, Cubs and Girl Guides made up the youngest group.

All these troops, or apprentice soldiers, were lined up where the parade had snaked to a halt around the wide boulevard in the heart of downtown Fort York. They surrounded the Cenotaph. In the very centre of the grass strip, circling the monument itself, stood the City Council and other dignitaries. A generous sprinkling of policemen, both uniformed and plainclothed, moved unobtrusively through the crowd. And, of course, there were many spectators.

Tretheway and Jake had stationed themselves close to F. McKnight Wakeley. Neither had a chance to talk at length to the Alderman but both commented on how unconcerned he appeared. But then, Tretheway thought, Wakeley never seems too concerned about anything.

The crowd grew quiet in anticipation of the eleventh hour. Tretheway scanned faces. At a sudden command from a leather-lunged Sergeant-Major, the parade jumped to attention. Even the city fathers stopped shuffling.

Fifty yards away, in the shadow of Sir John A. McDonald's statue, a young Sub-Lieutenant growled the order, "Fire!" One of two naval cannons, surrounded by kneeling Sea Cadets, leaped backwards with a roar that marked eleven o'clock exactly. Its echoes rebounded from building to building as the City Hall clock chimed the hour. The wind dispersed the cannon's smoke immediately. Flags dipped. All eyes, except policemen's, respectfully faced the ground. The silence seemed much longer than two minutes. Wind rattled the flag halliards. A street car bell clanged in the distance. Pigeons cooed. A young Cub Scout sneezed. Tretheway was aware of other policemen scanning the crowd.

A roar from the second cannon, marking the end of two minutes' silence, startled Tretheway. Five duty buglers brought five sterling silver ceremonial bugles to their lips. The Bugle-Major barked the order, "Sound!" The sad notes of the Last Post filled the frosty air. Officers saluted through the call and the following lonely piper's lament, dropping their arms only when the buglers began the Rouse.

Tretheway noticed a group of about thirty young spectators edging towards the Cenotaph. He grabbed Jake by the arm.

"Who the hell are they?"

"I don't know," Jake said.

At an unseen signal, the boys lined up quickly in orderly ranks of three and dramatically threw their coats off to reveal spanking white cassocks over vibrant, electric blue gowns. They began singing, "O Valiant Hearts".

"Jezuz!" Tretheway gasped.

"A choir," Jake said unnecessarily.

This was a signal for the wreath-laying to begin. The Lieutenant Governor of the Province laid the first. He was followed by the Mayor, several WWI veterans, a Silver Cross woman and other distinguished guests of the city. The choir finished their hymn, sang another and, when the ceremony was over, broke into "God Save the King".

When the RFYLI Chaplain came forward to give the Benediction, everyone knew the Armistice Day program was almost over.

Jake looked inquisitively at Tretheway.

Tretheway looked puzzled. "I don't think anything's going to happen."

"Nothing?" Jake said.

"It would've happened by now." Tretheway noticed Zulp through the crowd. He was craning his neck as though looking for something, or someone. His face seemed redder than usual. Jake saw him, too.

"I think the Chief . . ."

"I see him," Tretheway interrupted.

When the November murder did take place a week later, and the furore it caused had settled down a little, Jake tried, unsuccessfully, to console his boss.

"You said it would be Wakeley."

Tretheway nodded.

"And you said at the Cenotaph."

"I know."

"You were just a week early."

"You're batting .666."

"What's that mean?"

"You got two out of three."

"Then why didn't you say that?"

"Just baseball talk."

Tretheway didn't pursue the subject.

Following the Armistice ceremony, Tretheway had a terse one-sided discussion with Zulp while they were still at the Cenotaph.

"What about it, Tretheway?"

"Sir?"

"What happened?"

"Nothing."

"I know that. Why?"

"I don't know." Tretheway shook his head. "It should've."

"It should've! What kind of an excuse is that?"

"No excuse, Sir."

Zulp appeared at a loss for words, but just for a moment. He shook his finger as discreetly as possible under Tretheway's large nose. "The only thing that saves you is that hardly anybody knew about it. Like the *Expositor*. Secrecy. Security. Pays off."

Tretheway didn't answer. Zulp continued.

"Needless to say, you'll stick to traffic from now on."

Tretheway nodded.

"No more of this Thin Man crap." Zulp chuckled at his accidental humour. "And if you get any more ideas about this case, you come to me. Is that clear?"

"Yes, Sir." Tretheway turned to go.

"One more thing."

Tretheway turned back. Zulp smiled.

"Don't get any more ideas."

So Tretheway had immersed himself in traffic problems. For the next week, he checked traffic patterns and lights, commended the men who had written the most tickets—including the perennial champion, 'Two-book Cluett'—planned his radio safety show for December, made several court appearances and generally caught up on neglected paper work. The weekend arrived quickly.

Sunday was spent catching up on the war news in the *Expositor*. It reported that early in November Hermann Goering had ordered a change in policy. Throughout the week his German Luftwaffe had concentrated entirely on the night bombings of cities. That night the population of Fort York went to their safe beds while their hearts went out to the people of Coventry.

On Monday, the news was closer to home.

The initial alarm came from a wizened, puffy-faced man named Hercules who operated and lived in the Downtown Fort York Billiard Emporium across from the Cenotaph. According to the story he told Wan Ho, Hercules was awakened at approximately two a.m. by a number of regular bangs and one loud one. He ran to his second floor window and saw a dark figure, arms and legs stiffly outstretched, lying in the snow at the base of the monument. Far to the right, in the shadow of Sir John A. McDonald, Hercules thought he saw a group of blurry figures milling about suspiciously. But because of his daily intake of cheap sherry, blurry figures doing peculiar things were not too uncommon in Hercules' world.

Throwing a worn, stained parka over his long underwear and stepping into a pair of torn overshoes with broken buckles, he ran downstairs. As he approached the fallen figure, he saw that it was an army officer with a large service revolver clutched tightly in his right fist. And although Hercules didn't remember his name, he recognized him as the Alderman who usually wore a uniform and saluted a lot.

Hercules bent over the body far enough to detect a small black hole between Wakeley's eyes. He straightened up, shivering. More out of curiosity than courage, Hercules followed Wakeley's last footprints into the shadows toward Sir John. He circled the statue, but encountered no one. Someone, however, had scratched a message in the snow on the far side of the statue's base. Hercules read it, squinting the same way he did when he read wine labels. He didn't understand it, but it scared him badly anyway. Hercules ran, slipping, unsteady in his loose overshoes, across the street to what he had always thought was a police call box. When the Yellow Cab dispatcher at the other end of the line figured out what was going on, he relayed Hercules' call to the police. They responded in less than five minutes.

Tretheway was notified shortly after in the general alarm. By the time Jake had wheezed life into the Pontiac and he and Tretheway had driven in from the west end, the preliminary investigation was well under way. Most of Tretheway's information had to be gleaned from Wan Ho or his squad. Dr Nooner, who was almost getting used to his monthly emergency calls, had already been and gone, accompanying the body to the morgue for further examination. But he had left the pertinent medical facts with Wan Ho.

"Four bullets," Wan Ho said. "Probably small calibre. All in the upper body. Chest area."

"The report said several regular bangs and one loud one," Tretheway said. "I take it that was Wakeley's service revolver."

"Wakeley didn't fire back," Wan Ho said. "He tried. Doc Nooner said there was real pressure on the trigger."

"Then why . . ."

"His safety was on."

Tretheway looked puzzled.

"One more thing." Wan Ho pointed at the ground. "It looks like Wakeley walked back here, then turned around and was shot."

"While trying to fire his own gun?"

"Right. Here, look at this." Wan Ho walked beside Wakeley's footprints. Tretheway and Jake followed with two of Wan Ho's men. They stopped about halfway between the Cenotaph and Sir John A. McDonald. Wan Ho pointed down again. "There." Wakeley's tracks suddenly ran into a maze of other footprints that marred the snow the rest of the way to the statue. "It looks like several people."

"Maybe four or five?" Tretheway asked.

Wan Ho nodded. "They either stayed here and fired at Wakeley. Or walked back there," he pointed at the statue, "turned, like Wakeley did, and then fired."

"Like a duel?" Tretheway said.

"Like a duel," Wan Ho repeated.

"Damned unfair one," Jake said.

"Just a minute," Tretheway said.

They looked at him.

"Do you mean to tell me that early this morning at least five people, maybe more, had a duel with a city Alderman, shot him dead in downtown Fort York and nobody saw or heard anything? Where the hell were the beat men?"

"I know it sounds incredible," Wan Ho said. "But I've already checked with Central about the policemen on the downtown beat. And there is a hole in there. And it wouldn't be too difficult to find out when. Ask a few questions. Watch a few nights." Wan Ho looked at Tretheway. "You should know the police can't be there every minute."

Tretheway agreed grudgingly.

"So for over a quarter hour," Wan Ho went on, "if there was no other traffic—and Sunday night is usually quiet—they'd have clear sailing."

"They took an awful chance," Jake said.

"They did with every murder," Tretheway said.

"You're right," Wan Ho said. "But this time, there's a witness."

Tretheway started. "Who? Where is he?"

"Over there." Wan Ho inclined his head toward an official car parked across the street. "In Zulp's car. His name's Hercules . . . ah . . ."

One of Wan Ho's men produced a notebook. "Goodfellow. Hercules Goodfellow." He pointed to the second storey poolroom. "His observations were made from up there."

"That's Herc's place," Jake blurted out. "The poolroom."

"Do you know him?" Wan Ho asked.

"Sort of."

"You play pool?" Tretheway asked, surprised.

"Maybe a little English billiards," Jake apologized. "Only sometimes."

"Is this Hercules reliable, Jake?" Wan Ho asked.

"I'd hate to go to court with him," Jake said. "He drinks a bit."

"That's what I thought," Wan Ho said.

"Did you talk to him before Zulp took him away?" Tretheway asked Wan Ho.

"Yes. Long enough." Wan Ho took five minutes to relate all the details of Hercules' story. "And he's a little vague about everything except the message written in the snow," he concluded.

"What'd it say?" Tretheway asked.

"You'd better look first," Wan Ho said.

They followed him around to the far side of Sir John. Wan Ho shone his flashlight at the statue's base, now clear of snow. "There," he said. "The message was there, he said."

"He said?" Tretheway questioned. "You never saw it?"

"No," Wan Ho said. "It could've blown away."

"You mean, if it was ever there."

"That's true."

"And he remembers what it said?"

"Word for word." Wan Ho flicked a finger at one of his men. Tretheway and Jake waited while the detective flipped through his book again. He cleared his throat before speaking. "War is nothing but a duel on an extensive scale."

After a few seconds, Tretheway broke the silence. "Now what the hell does that mean?"

Wan Ho spread his arms in ignorance.

"This Hercules remembered that?"

"Can't shake him," Wan Ho said.

"I'm surprised he could read it," Jake said.

"Another thing," Tretheway said. "What's the occasion?"

"Pardon?" Wan Ho went blank.

"The special day. The holiday. What's November 18?" Tretheway turned to Jake. "Do you know?"

"Ah . . . not offhand. The first was All Saints' Day. Last Monday was Armistice." Jake thought for a moment. "End of the month is St. Andrew's Day. But the eighteenth . . ." He shook his head.

"Any ideas, Wan Ho?" Tretheway asked.

"No," Wan Ho answered. "I'm really in the dark on this one."

"I think we're about to be enlightened," Jake said, craning his neck and peering around Tretheway in the direction of Zulp's car. They all turned to see Zulp approaching with Hercules Goodfellow in tow. Zulp was smiling.

"How's it going, Sergeant?" he asked.

"Fine, Sir," Wan Ho answered. "Just going over the facts."

Zulp stopped smiling when he saw Tretheway. "What are you doing here?"

"General alarm," Tretheway said.

"Oh. All right, then." Zulp seemed unsure of himself. "You were seven days out, you know."

"Yes, Sir."

"And I suppose you have a theory about this?"

"No, Sir."

"Well, then." Zulp's confidence strengthened. "If you'd all pay attention."

The group tried to look more attentive.

"I've been interrogating our star witness here." Zulp indicated Hercules, who was enjoying being the centre of attention. "And I've come up with a few facts. Ideas. Solutions. Thought we should discuss them. Feel free to add your own." He glanced at Tretheway. "Within reason. Now. First." He clasped his hands behind his back and appeared to stare at the sky. "Does anybody know who owns that place?"

No one answered right away.

"Ah . . . what place?" Wan Ho asked finally.

Zulp lowered his eyes and pointed across the street.

"There. That place. The poolroom. Where Mr Goodfellow works."

Hercules nodded adamantly in agreement.

"No," Wan Ho said. His two men said the same thing.

Tretheway and Jake shook their heads.

"Pennylegion. Joseph Pennylegion." Zulp waited a dramatic moment so the startling revelation could sink in before he went on. "The Controller!"

Nobody said anything again.

"Well," Zulp urged. "How about that?"

"I didn't know that," Wan Ho said.

"Neither did I," Tretheway said. "But what's it got to do with Wakeley's murder?"

"The observation point. Mr Goodfellow here, saw almost the whole thing from up there." Zulp pointed again. Hercules nodded adamantly again.

"Yes. But how does that tie in?" Tretheway asked.

"You know Pennylegion's lifestyle." Zulp looked around the group. "Unsavoury companions. Dark shirts. White ties. The funny names. Big cars. This was obviously a gangland-style killing."

"With twenty-twos?" Tretheway asked.

"What the hell's the difference?" Zulp shouted. "Who cares about calibre?"

"It's just that you associate gangland stuff with shotguns," Wan Ho intervened. "Or machine guns. And more violence."

"Murder isn't violent?" Zulp asked.

"But I still don't see the connection," Tretheway said.

"Why not?" Zulp said. "He's a politician."

"We can't arrest him for that," Tretheway said. "Or because he has a poolroom."

"He owns seven of them," Zulp countered.

"That's still no crime," Tretheway said.

"And I'll wager that today is an occasion." Zulp ignored Tretheway. "A special day. A meaningful one to the criminal element. Like John Dillinger's birthday. Or the founding of Alcatraz. Or even some anniversary of the Fort York Jail."

"But what's it prove?" Tretheway persisted.

"Dammit, Tretheway! Use your head. Think of something. Imagination." Zulp turned to the others. "I can't do everything for you. I've given you the germ. The nucleus. Make it grow. Run it down. Like good policemen." He was distracted by the approach of the *Fort York Expositor's* star reporter and a camera-man. "Here comes trouble," Zulp said under his breath. "Let's get on with the job. Remember. Mum's the word again." He straightened his hat and pulled his tunic into place before he turned to face the intruders.

The investigation proceeded routinely—or as routinely as a sixth murder in as many months could. Hercules Goodfellow had a field day telling his story to the press. His actions became braver and his deductions more profound with each retelling of the events.

By now, the police knew what to do without being told. Uniformed men cordoned off the whole park. Wan Ho's squad searched the ground thoroughly for more footprints, fingerprints, and clues of any importance, while other detectives went, once again, door-to-door seeking information. Squad cars patrolled in ever-widening circles around the area. Zulp kept appearing at different vantage points with unnecessary commands.

Tretheway, meanwhile, walked the periphery of the park with Jake beside him. He had been put in charge of the uniformed men stationed around, but away from, the murder scene—an inspirational last minute assignment from Chief Zulp.

"I wonder if they've found anything?" Tretheway said.

"We'll never know from here," Jake complained.

Despite all the activity, no other new, or startling, information turned up. By the time the sun rose to herald a new work week for the citizens of Fort York, most of the policemen, including Tretheway and Jake, had been sent home. Addie met them at the front door.

"Let me take your coats," she said. "You look perished."

"That's not the greatest heating system you've got in that car," Tretheway complained.

"The roof's a little drafty," Jake defended.

Addie hung their coats up on the hall stand. They both laid their fur hats on the top of Tretheway's trophy cabinet.

"How about some hot tea?" Addie offered.

"Love it, Addie," Jake said.

"But not with that mob." Tretheway referred to the breakfast noises coming from the kitchen and dining rooms. Students with early morning classes were noisily eating porridge, toast, eggs, waffles and anything else Addie had prepared for the morning meal.

"In here." Addie pulled apart the sliding parlour doors. "I'll bring some toast in with the tea."

Tretheway and Jake glanced uncertainly at each other. "Addie," Jake began.

"I heard about Major-General Wakeley on the radio," she said.

"Oh," Jake said.

"And I think it's just terrible." Addie's lip trembled. "What's going to happen?"

"Don't you worry, Addie," Jake said.

"But I do!" Addie grabbed Jake by the arm. "It just can't go on and on. I'm really afraid this time."

"Well . . ." Jake tried to think of something reassuring to say.

"There won't be any more, Addie," Tretheway said.

"Pardon?" Addie said.

Jake looked just as surprised as Addie, but didn't say anything.

"I said there won't be any more killings." Tretheway locked eyes with his sister. "That's a promise."

"But . . ." Addie began.

"Addie," Tretheway said, "if you want to worry about something, worry about the tea."

"Well . . ." Addie let go of Jake's arm and looked down self-consciously as she straightened the front of her dress. "Oh," she remembered suddenly, "Wan Ho called." She took the message from her pocket and read aloud. "Medical Report. Three small calibre 22's. One large calibre tentatively identified as WWI Mauser pistol . . ." She looked up. "Does that make sense?"

"The big bang." Tretheway brightened.

Addie started for the kitchen. "I'll bring in some hot buttered buns, too. You look starved."

The thought of Tretheway looking starved made Jake chuckle to himself. He was tempted to ask about the "no-more-killings" remark, but refrained. Over the years Jake had learned that if Tretheway wanted to tell him something, he'd do it in his own good time—and probably tell him before anyone else—but asking or prodding didn't hurry the process.

For the next two weeks, Tretheway was noticeably quiet. He went upstairs to his own room earlier than usual, spent more time sitting back in his oversized chair puffing smoke rings at the ceiling and, although not grouchy, used no more words than necessary when forced into a conversation. The only time he came slightly out of his shell was when word reached him of Zulp's new theory.

Apparently when Chief Zulp was researching November 18, he stumbled on, or in his words was guided to, the fact that Sir William Schwenck Gilbert was born on this day. And that this was the Gilbert of Gilbert and Sullivan who wrote, among other things, *The Pirates of Penzance*. One of the most popular songs from the operetta and Zulp's favourite was "I am the Very Model of a Modern Major-General." The fact that Wakeley held the same unusual rank in the Cadet Corps was enough to excite Zulp into forgetting, or at least putting aside, the John Dillinger Birthday Theory.

"And now it's my job to find some sort of tie-in," Wan Ho moaned. He was in the traffic office where he had come to tell Tretheway the latest turn of events.

Tretheway laughed out loud. "Like he was killed by a travelling Gilbert and Sullivan chorus?"

"Or sung to death," Jake suggested.

Wan Ho had to smile. "Our Chief huge reservoir of irrelevance," he said in his best Charlie Chan imitation. Wan Ho folded his hands across his stomach and bowed stiffly. "Thank you so much."

Tretheway's good mood lasted the rest of the day, but the next morning he was as sombre as before. He continued so into December.

DECEMBER

On Wednesday morning, exactly two weeks before Christmas Day, Tretheway made a short announcement without lifting his eyes from the breakfast table.

"I've got some thinking to do. It might take some time. I'll be upstairs." He looked up at a surprised Addie. "I'd appreciate it if you'd send my lunch up. And maybe dinner." He pushed his chair back.

"But . . . what about work?" Addie asked.

"I've got some sick leave coming." Tretheway pushed his way out the swinging door.

Addie and Jake listened while the sounds of Tretheway's footsteps disappeared up the stairs.

"Well," Addie said. "What do you make of that?"

"Just what he said," Jake said. "He's got some thinking to do."

"Should I call Dr Nooner?" she asked.

"No. Leave him be, Addie." Jake stood up. "I'll look in on him tonight."

As it worked out, Jake had to alibi for his boss for the next three days. He coped with all the paper work he could manage and hoped that the department would more or less run itself temporarily.

Addie inveigled some students to run Tretheway's meals upstairs four times a day. Tretheway acknowledged their services with a curt but civil grunt at his door. Between meals, he would bellow from his doorway for different things—an encyclopedia, the 'C' volume of the *Book of Knowledge,* an obscure history book of Jake's—which were also run upstairs. But mainly, he stayed in his room.

At one point, Addie tip-toed to the door and listened. She was rewarded only by the sound of chalk squeaking on a blackboard, low mutterings, pages turning briskly and, just before she went back downstairs, the unmistakeable pop of a bottle top. Finally, on Friday night, Tretheway ended his self-imposed quarantine.

135

Jake and Addie were making themselves as comfortable as possible, under the circumstances, in the parlour. Tea was brewing on the wheeled table. The radio was tuned to the NBC Red Network in anticipation of "The Amos and Andy Show". Faint noises came from the kitchen where some of the boarders were cleaning up and finishing the dishes for Addie. It was relatively quiet. The students who hadn't gone home for Christmas were studying for the last of the exams. O. Pitts, though, had announced that he wasn't going anywhere for the holidays, so Addie had invited him for Christmas dinner and to the New Year's Eve party. It was just as well, she thought, that her brother was upstairs. He would find out soon enough about O. Pitts.

When the first bars of the "Amos and Andy" theme song floated over the air waves and the Westminster chimes of the mantel clock marked seven o'clock, Tretheway dramatically pulled open the doors of the parlour.

"Albert!" Addie said. "You gave me quite a start."

"Hi, Boss," Jake said, with genuine relief.

Tretheway's face shone from a recent shave. His hair was neatly brilliantined into place. He looked pleased with himself. Stretched across his chest, on a freshly-laundered white sweat shirt were the words "Individual Champion Empire Games 1928."

"Addie, Jake," he said in quiet greeting. "Is there any tea left?"

"Certainly." Addie pushed forward in her chair. "Your mug's on the trolley."

"Don't get up." Tretheway poured himself half a mugful and carried it back to his chair.

"Everything all right?" Jake said. "Is there . . ."

Tretheway held up his hand in a gesture perfected by thirteen years of directing traffic. "Let's hear 'Amos and Andy'."

For the next thirty minutes, they smiled, chuckled and belly laughed through the blackface comedy program. At least Tretheway and Addie did. Jake recalled later that, although he had laughed along with Tretheway and Addie, he couldn't remember one funny line, situation or joke in the whole show. At the end of the program, which seemed interminable to Jake, Tretheway was ready to talk.

"Jake."

"Hm?" Jake perked up.

"I'd like to go over a few thoughts with you. About the case."

"Sure," Jake said. "Anytime."

"It might take an hour."

"That's all right."

"Or two."

"There's nothing on the radio anyway."

"Let's go." Tretheway stood up. "If you'll excuse us, Addie."

Addie wrinkled her forehead.

"Don't look so worried," Jake said. "Everything'll be all right."

Addie looked questioningly at Tretheway. He nodded.

Inside Tretheway's quarters, Jake was struck once again by the warm, intimate atmosphere. He had been there before and his reaction was always the same. On the one hand, Jake enjoyed the relaxed and interesting surroundings, but, on the other, he felt as though he was prying into Tretheway's private life.

It was a high-ceilinged, spacious room, decorated in muted browns, on the second floor corner. There were two recessed nooks on either side of the door that couldn't be seen until you had gone into the room and turned around. The one on the left held Tretheway's roll-top desk, a swivel chair and a floor-to-ceiling built-in bookcase. Many contemporary whodunits, Shakespeare's tragedies and a complete set of law books jammed the shelves. On the right hand side, behind a closed door, Jake knew there was a bathroom. It contained the usual toilet and sink, but because of a previous embarrassing experience, similar to the rumble seat episode, Tretheway had replaced the bathtub with an elaborate, king-sized shower stall.

Directly opposite the door was Tretheway's impressive over-sized bed. To one side of it, by a large window, stood an eight-drawer dresser, side table, lamp and straight chair. On the other side, by another large window, was Tretheway's favourite orange chair with matching footstool and a small table that held some magazines, a humidor of cigars and a souvenir ashtray made from a World War I artillery shell.

The room would have been symmetrical if it were not for a curtained recess beside the orange chair. Tonight the curtain was open, revealing a small counter and cupboards flanking an ice-box that held Molson Blue and several old cheeses. On the counter top rested a toaster, a single hot plate and the makings for tea.

Near Tretheway's bed hung a group of framed photographs.

Addie appeared in a couple—once alone and once with an older couple who Jake assumed were the elder Tretheways. A picture of a ridiculously young, khaki-clad soldier, with two wound stripes on his sleeve, showed Tretheway in earlier days. Several pictures of policemen, at ease and in uniform, shared the gallery with some of Tretheway's track and field companions. There was one picture, no larger or more colourful than the rest, that dominated the grouping. In a simple, oval frame was a soft-focus sepia print of a girl in her early twenties. Her hauntingly beautiful eyes demanded your attention. Jake had never asked about her and Tretheway had never volunteered an explanation.

The room boasted the unusual luxury of an open fireplace. Overall, a mixture of fresh linen, cigar smoke, burning applewood and Yardley's after shave provided a pleasant aroma.

"Make yourself comfortable, Jake." Tretheway handed Jake a beer and popped one for himself. He dragged a blackboard into the centre of the room.

Jake sat down on the bed, then realized that because of the two mattresses and double sets of springs, his legs dangled uncomfortably over the edge like a young child's in a high chair. He climbed down, decided against being engulfed in the orange chair and took a few tentative squats on the footstool.

"Dammit, Jake. Sit down." Tretheway said.

Jake settled for a straight chair in front of the blackboard. He crossed his legs and looked attentive. Tretheway began.

"The first three, or really four happenings, were trial balloons. Tests. Experiments." He wagged his finger at Jake for emphasis. "And practice."

Jake raised his hand uncertainly.

"What is it?" Tretheway asked.

"Is it all right to ask questions?"

Tretheway thought for a moment. "It might even help," he said. "Do you have one?"

"Yes." Jake stood up. "When you say the first three or four, do you mean starting at February? Or is the piece of coal thing one of them?"

"You don't have to stand up," Tretheway said. Jake sat down. "But you're right. New Year's Day was the first one." He picked up a giant night stick—a souvenir piece covered with pen and ink signatures that his division had given him—to use as a pointer.

"This case has a logic, even a rhythm to it. As I've said before, a pattern. There are things we're supposed to see, such as the ceremony, or rituals. And there are things we're not supposed to see, like the mistakes."

Tretheway tapped the blackboard with this stick. He had chalked the left half into twelve squares with neat, but hard-to-read, scrawls in each space. The right half was blank.

"I've marked the board, here, into twelve months. And as you can see, I've written in the holiday and any pertinent facts for each one."

Jake looked puzzled.

"You can't see," Tretheway stated.

Jake shook his head.

"Very well." Tretheway pointed at the first square. "This is January. It says Gum. New Year's Day. Coal."

"I see," Jake said.

"The holiday was New Year's Day. Not New Year's Eve. And the piece of coal is what I mean by ceremony. In this case, a European custom that says, to bring luck, the first visitor to a home in the new year must be of dark complexion. That is, not blonde. And bear a gift. The traditional gift being a piece of coal. And you've never heard of that?"

Jake shook his head again. Tretheway shrugged.

"It doesn't seem like much by itself, but I'm convinced it was well-planned. There's the element of boldness about it. Chance-taking. Illegal entry. I'll bet they all went in. A dark one first. That's trespass. But if they'd been caught it would've been laughed off. A joke. No harm done. Especially after a New Year's Eve party. But they weren't caught. They got away with it."

"Why a holiday?" Jake asked.

"Arbitrary. A good choice, really. But basically a red herring. A vehicle. A better question would be, why *not* a holiday? Gave them something to plan around. And don't forget, the first four, or even five, could've been laughed off as pranks. And at the same time, it was a perfect cover-up for their real purpose."

"Which was?"

"As old as time." Tretheway held his hand up. "But let's be as logical as they are. Don't rush things."

Tretheway downed the last of his beer bottle. He went to the ice-box. "You ready, Jake?"

Jake took a two-handed pull from his own bottle and choked. He coughed and sputtered. "Wrong way," he whispered hoarsely. He held his hand up and shook his head.

Tretheway popped another bottle and came back to the blackboard.

"Now you have a group who've pulled off their first experiment successfully. What do they do now?" Tretheway didn't wait for, or expect, an answer. "Valentine's Day. A little riskier. A little more elaborate. The chicken's not important, but the arrow through the heart is. That's the ceremony. A symbol of love. And the name of the recipient? Valentini. Perfect. And remember what she said? A delivery man handed it to her. She couldn't describe him but everyone knows her eyesight is terrible. She said there was a van parked at the curb. I'll bet the rest of them were in it. And if they'd been caught, which they weren't, it was just a prank again. A little more serious, but not criminal."

"Wait a minute," Jake interrupted. Beer always gave him confidence. "You mean Mrs Valentini was that close to the murderer?"

"It's my guess he handed her the package."

"He?"

"That's right."

"Not a woman?"

"I don't think a woman would send a valentine to another woman. An improper ceremony. Not traditional."

Jake thought for a moment. "And how come he picks politicians? Another red herring?"

"No. That was all part of his plan. And in March," Tretheway continued without further explanation, "the boldness escalated again." He pointed to the third square. "St. Patrick's Day. Emmett O'Dell. Poodles. The logistics were more complicated. Getting the green dye there. Sneaking around the back yard at night. The ceremony of dunking the dogs. A lot more risk. Good practice for greater things. But still no real harm. And a good tie-in. I mean, have you heard of a more Irish name than O'Dell?"

Jake nodded. "And they got away again."

"Exactly. And the same deal in April." Tretheway deciphered his scrawlings in the next square. "April Fool's. Fire. Mayor Trutt. And another great tie-in. The Mayor used to be a fireman. Everyone knew he was afraid of fire. And more than one person calls him a fool." Tretheway put his beer bottle down and wiped his wet palms on his sweatshirt. "The hanging jester was a nice piece of ceremony. And the choice of time was interesting. Just before dawn. I'm convinced that was to accommodate the *FY Expositor* photographer. That's nerve. Bold." Tretheway pointed his night stick at Jake. "There'd be less risk at, say, midnight. Or two in the morning."

"You're right," Jake said.

"May twenty-fourth. Queen's birthday. Firecrackers. Mac." Tretheway smacked the palm of his free hand with the night stick several times.

"Don't smear the signatures," Jake said.

"Eh?"

Jake pointed at the night stick.

"Oh." Tretheway took the baton out of his hand and examined it carefully. "It doesn't fit."

"What?" Jake said.

"I've said it before. The twenty-fourth of May doesn't fit the pattern. There wasn't that much risk. No particular boldness required. No ceremony. How could he be sure Mac would light the fire? And what's the tie-in with the Queen's birthday?" Tretheway smacked hs palm again. "No. It didn't come off."

"Do you know why?" Jake asked.

"I have an idea," Tretheway said.

Jake waited. Tretheway turned to the blackboard again. "But they sure as hell made up for it." He smacked the next month with his stick. "June. Father's Day. Father Cosentino. They graduate into murder. Big time. Ceremony bolder than ever. Strangled with a typical Father's Day gift. Fits the pattern perfectly. This time, they had to get away with it. And they did."

Jake waited for Tretheway to settle down before he asked a question. "Does religion enter into it? I mean, with Father Cosentino being a priest?"

"No. I don't think so." Tretheway exchanged his night stick for a piece of chalk. "Now, let's write down what we know for sure. And things we were supposed to see." He translated aloud as he scribbled on the blank right hand half of the blackboard. "Killer strikes on holidays. Victims—politicians. Specifically FY City Council. Careful planning. Imaginative. Bold."

He looked at Jake. "Think of anything else?"

Jake shook his head. Tretheway drew a double line under his notations.

"And now the things we're not supposed to see. The mistakes." He bent down to the board again. "Male," Tretheway said as he wrote. "That much we learned, or surmised from St. Valentine's Day." He wrote again. "And more than one. That was confirmed by Dr Nooner on Father's Day." He straightened up. "Now in July, he started to get tricky." Tretheway poked his ear thoughtfully with the piece of chalk. "The holidays so far had been pretty legitimate. Regular. Run of the mill. Predictable holidays. And I still say Dominion Day, July first, was the next logical choice."

"Then why . . ."

"Maybe just for that reason. Too obvious. Maybe he knew that we knew. Everyone was ready for it. Prepared. There's a fine line between boldness and bravado. So when he didn't strike on Dominion Day, we thought that was the end of it. Remember Zulp's theory that all events climaxed with Cosentino's murder? Sounded reasonable. Then he surprised us on July fifteenth." Tretheway shook his head. "St. Swithin's Day. Who the hell ever heard of St. Swithin's Day?"

"Addie did," Jake said.

"I know that now," Tretheway snapped. "And it had all the usual tie-ins. Miss Tommerup was the closest to a Viking on City Council. The Rain Saint. The rain barrel. Hell, it even rained that day. Probably during the murder. The ceremony."

Jake shuddered.

"But there was one thing we weren't supposed to see," Tretheway went on. "The mistake."

"What's that?"

Tretheway turned back to his list. "Maltese Cross," he said as he wrote. "Remember? Pressed into Ingird Tommerup's leg."

Jake winced as he nodded.

"By itself, not too significant. But put them all together . . ." Tretheway trailed off. He finished his second Molson. Jake drained his first. Tretheway took a beer from the ice-box and brought Jake another without asking.

"Civic Holiday next," Tretheway said. "Caught us off guard again. A regular holiday this time. Remember Zulp spreading the word about St. Bartholomew's Day? Poor little Henry Plain. Not an elected official, but very important to the running of city government. The head civic employee. There's your obvious neat tie-in. Smothered in paper. An inspiration. How often had you heard Henry say that?"

"His favourite saying," Jake said.

"Bold. Daring. Well-planned but not perfect."

"What was their mistake?" Jake asked.

"Pointed heads." Tretheway scribbled on the blackboard. "We weren't supposed to see. A mistake. Small, but a mistake."

"What's it mean?"

"Wait'll we get them all together." Tretheway picked up the night stick in his free hand. He tapped the blackboard. "That was August. Now September. Everybody breathed easier after Labour Day. An unusual holiday. But perfect casting. Lucifer skewered with a flaming sword. Dramatic. Just like the legend. Obvious. The daisies spread around. The ceremony more elaborate, but again climaxing with murder. Everything out in the open for all to see."

"What weren't we supposed to see?"

"Hear," Tretheway corrected. "And this time, we didn't find out till Morgan told us."

"Told us what?"

"The organ music. Remember? God bless Morgan for recognizing Wagner."

"How does that fit in?"

"In a minute." Tretheway chalked the composer's name in at the bottom of the list.

"Don't you think Morgan killed Taz?" Jake asked.

Tretheway shook his head. "He stumbled into it."

"But . . ." Jake began.

"Patience, Jake." Tretheway poked his night stick at October. "Hallowe'en. The perfect night for a murder. Dark and spooky. They were in costume. Perfect cover if anybody saw them. Ammerman did, up close. He was too old and they knew it. They ran him. Threatened him. And scared him to death. The boldness was there again. But this time, they had dumb luck on their side."

"You mean in the woods?"

"Yes. The sassafras leaves puts them at the Point. If we'd had the luck, old Ammerman might still be with us."

"I know," Jake said. "And what about that spearhead we found? Does that figure at all?"

"Yes," Tretheway said. "Definitely. A bonus. But it's not a spearhead."

"What is it?"

"The top part of a pickelhaube," Tretheway said.

"Pickle what?"

Without any further explanation, Tretheway legibly printed the word PICKELHAUBE on the blackboard. He put the chalk down along with the night stick. Taking one of his giant cigars from the humidor, he twirled it between his lips, then deliberately lit the business end. Clouds of smoke surrounded his head.

"The eighteenth of November." Tretheway blew the smoke away. "That's the key date, Jake. That's the one that tightens the weave. Binds the cheese. Straightens the horizon, so to speak."

"Nothing to do with Gilbert and Sullivan?" Jake chuckled.

"No." Tretheway smiled and shook his head. "Nor with the underworld."

"Then what was it?"

"On November the eighteenth, 1931, Karl Von Clausewitz died." Tretheway blew several smoke rings in the air. "Does that mean anything to you?"

Jake looked blank.

"Dammit, Jake." Tretheway prompted. "You're the college man. Didn't you major in history?"

"Wait a minute." Jake's blankness disappeared. "German writer."

"Prussian," Tretheway corrected.

"That's right. Ah . . . military writer. Wrote on the science, or art, of war. Certainly. He actually fought against Napoleon. *On War* was the name of his best known work. Tremendous strategist. Very influential. Even today he's studied for military tactics."

"That's the one," Tretheway said. "He was big on total war. War on citizens, territory or property. Anything goes."

"But why Clausewitz?" Jake asked.

Tretheway thought for a moment. "Everybody has an idol. Shakespeare, Roosevelt, Churchill, Pasteur."

"Syl Apps, Lawson Little," Jake interrupted.

Tretheway frowned and went on. "Suppose for some reason, our man's idol was Clausewitz. Maybe he discovered him when he was young. Maybe he just fell into an open slot in the murderer's philosophy. But, anyway, suppose Clausewitz became his patron saint or leader. There are books available about him in every library in Canada. It's hard to find a writer on warfare in the last hundred years who hasn't quoted—or misquoted—Clausewitz somewhere in his work. And these quotes—mind you most of them are out of context—are very interesting."

"Oh?"

"Listen to what he says about being nervy. 'Boldness is the stamp of a hero.' He says more, but that shows his position."

"Obviously, he thought boldness was a good thing," Jake said.

"Undoubtedly," Tretheway said. "And he doesn't mind killing people. 'Let us not hear of generals who conquer without bloodshed.' How did you like that?"

"Does our killer consider himself a general?" Jake said.

"Yes. Or, at least a leader. There are all sorts of other quotes, but listen to this one. His most famous. I think it tells us something about the murderer." Tretheway cleared is throat. " 'War is a mere continuance of political policy by another means.' "

"You mean . . ." Jake started.

"I mean that our man is a politician first. A killer second. The murders were merely an extension of a political belief."

"What political belief?"

"German."

"But . . ."

"Check the list." Tretheway threw his cigar in the fireplace and retrieved his chalk and night stick. He banged the blackboard. "We have a leader, or general if you prefer, and a group of followers. Extremely loyal followers. 'There is nothing in war that is of greater importance than obedience.' There's one I forgot."

Tretheway drew a line through the word "Maltese" and scribbled something else over it. "Change Maltese to Iron Cross. Same shape. A German wartime decoration for bravery. Next!"

He smacked the board for emphasis.

"The music Morgan heard. Wagner. German composer. Clausewitz's favourite."

Tretheway pushed his hand into his pocket and brought out the pointed metal object found on the floor of the garden hut. The flickering light from the fireplace danced on the metal spike as Tretheway held it at arm's length. "A pickelhaube is a Prussian steel helmet. The very symbol of Prussian and German armed might for years. You remember. The Kaiser wore one. They couldn't make a move about the First World War without one. And this is the spike from the top of a pickelhaube. A pointed head."

Tretheway put the broken spike down and went immediately into November.

"And I don't have to remind you of the Wakeley killing. Boldness. They could've been discovered. Or shot. They didn't know poor old Wakeley would forget about his safety catch. And a Mauser's a German pistol. Our man may be a bad shot, but as the leader he had the biggest gun. And the ceremony. You can guess who said, 'War is nothing . . .' "

". . .'but a duel on an extensive scale,' " Jake finished. "Clausewitz."

The two men sat quietly for a minute. Jake recklessly finished his beer. Tretheway drained his bottle. He looked at Jake questioningly. Jake nodded. Tretheway went to the ice-box and took out two more quarts.

"Let's take these downstairs and heat up some of Addie's rhubarb pie," Tretheway suggested. He stood up.

"Right." Jake rose unsteadily. "One thing first though. These people, hell, the enemy. Are they trying to take over the government? The Fort York government?"

"Disrupt," Tretheway corrected. "Completely disrupt is a better way of putting it. Haven't you noticed things slowing down at City Hall? The Council's not running as smoothly as before. They're planning a by-election shortly, but there are five people missing right now. Six, counting Henry Plain."

"So the killer's plan is working."

"Let's just hope it's not going on in every Canadian city."

"Do you know . . ." Jake stopped, then started again. "Do you know who it is?"

"I think so." There was a trace of sadness in Tretheway's voice.

The forbidding evil visions and unanswered questions that whirled around Jake's head that night played second fiddle to the effects of the unaccustomed three quarts of beer. He slept well, or at least deeply. When Jake finally reached the breakfast table on Saturday morning, he learned that Tretheway had already left the house.

"Where'd he go, Addie?" Jake asked.

"He walked over to King Street. Christmas shopping, he said."

For the rest of the day, Jake helped Addie around the house, stripping beds, picking up rooms and moving furniture out of her sweeper's way. It was a busy time of year for the boarding house. All the servicemen and students except O. Pitts would be gone by next weekend—the weekend before Christmas. Every night there were impromptu farewell parties with their tearful, if temporary, goodbyes. Addie remembered all her boarders with a knitted something—tea cosy, muffler, diamond socks—while they reciprocated mainly with potted plants.

During the following week, Jake had little time to ask Tretheway about the next holiday, what with his own Christmas shopping and the unavoidable turkey rolls and parties. And Tretheway had not encouraged any discussion. On the Monday before Christmas, the twenty-third, Jake finally broached the subject.

It was late evening. Jake was in the cellar watching Tretheway shovel coal into the furnace. The two of them and Addie had just returned from the Annual Police Christmas Concert. Tretheway sang every year with the police chorus and this Christmas his patriotic, rich baritone rendition of "Land of Hope and Glory" had knocked the audience, mostly policemen, out of their seats. Their applause demanded more. Tretheway encored with a tender, unaccompanied version of a contemporary favourite, "Love Walked In". There wasn't a dry eye in the house.

Tretheway hummed the same song now as Jake watched him manhandle large shovelfuls of coal into the furnace's fiery opening like so many spoonfuls of sugar.

"Nice tune," Jake said.

"Good melody," Tretheway agreed.

"Should I be worried?"

"Eh?" Tretheway stopped shovelling.

"About the next holiday," Jake said. "I'm sorry, but I've some questions."

Tretheway flung one last shovelful of coal into the furnace then slammed the door. "Like what?"

"You don't have to tell me who the killer is."

"Go on."

"But when will it happen? Christmas is coming. Who's the victim? I think I should know."

"You're right." Tretheway put the shovel down. "I was going to tell you. Now's as good a time as any."

Jake dusted off an old kitchen chair. He sat down and crossed his legs.

"Enjoy Christmas," Tretheway said. "I'd say New Year's Eve. That's the time. And right here. That's the place."

"Here? In the basement?"

"In the house, somewhere."

"But we'll be here. And Wan Ho. And Zulp. And the whole bloody City Council . . ."

" 'Boldness is the stamp of a hero'," Tretheway quoted.

Jake was beginning to regret his questions. "What about the victim? Who do you think it'll be?"

"This is a biggie."

"Eh?" Jake definitely felt uneasy.

"This is the last one. The coup de grace. The end of the year. I think he'll go for the bundle."

"The bundle?" Jake went white.

"The whole City Council. Or, at least, as many as possible."

"But how?"

"That I don't know. How would you do it?"

"Eh?"

"How would you get rid of a bunch of people? In one place? At a New Year's Eve party?"

"I don't know." Jake thought for a moment. "Food poisoning?"

"I never thought of that." Tretheway looked troubled.

"Just a suggestion."

"Tea's ready, Jake!" Addie shouted from the top of the cellar stairs. She knew there was no sense in asking Tretheway if he wanted tea after the sun had dipped under the yardarm. "And there's some fresh cake if you want it."

"No cake, Addie," Jake answered a little too fast. He smiled self-consciously at Tretheway. "I'm just not hungry."

Christmas itself was a quiet time for the Tretheways. With the exception of O. Pitts, all of the boarders were absent. It was a period of recuperative calm compared with the regular frantic University semesters.

On Christmas Eve, Fred the Labrador's owners dropped in with

Fred for a quick drink and ended up carolling around the piano. Tretheway's voice was, of course, the strongest and led the group, while Jake's and Addie's blended pleasantly together in the background. The neighbours sang adequately because they were church people. O. Pitts' enthusiasm almost made up for his tone deafness.

Christmas morning, Tretheway rose early, as he did every year, and roused the others. Then he, Jake, Addie, and O. Pitts sat around the Christmas tree in the sunroom and exchanged presents before breakfast.

Tretheway gave Addie a giant gift package of Evening in Paris cosmetics, a large garish, glamour pin—that she'd probably store away in her drawer with the other heavy jewellery Tretheway favoured—and some cash. Addie gave Tretheway a maroon smoking jacket with black satin lapels that she said would be much more comfortable than his old sweat shirts. Jake and Addie exchanged cashmere sweaters. Tretheway thought they were too expensive and too personal, but he didn't say anything.

Other gifts between the four of them included playing cards, cigars, books, whiskey, ties, socks and handkerchiefs. A mystery package under the tree turned out to be a huge red dish for Fred the Labrador that Tretheway had bought and wrapped himself. O. Pitts gave Jake and Addie each a small Bible.

For some reason, he gave Tretheway a joke book.

The gift-giving and the sumptuous Christmas dinner that followed helped keep their thoughts away from the Holiday Killer. Besides, Addie said to herself, nothing bad ever happens on Christmas Day. But when Christmas passed and then the weekend, they all girded themselves mentally for the end of the year.

On Monday, the day before the New Year's Eve party, Jake noticed his boss carrying a number of books towards the stairs. He watched while Tretheway put them on the hall table and went into the parlour. Jake, ostensibly examining his features in the hall mirror, sneaked a look at the titles. Tretheway appeared suddenly with half a cigar he had retrieved from the parlour ashtray. "Mirror, mirror, on the wall, eh Jake?" He snatched his books from the table and went upstairs to his room, but not before Jake had managed to see some titles: *The Dangerous Properties of Industrial Explosives, Poison Parade, Asphyxiating and Lethal Gases, The Microbe in Warfare,* and one entitled simply, *Massacres.*

At eight o'clock on New Year's Eve, Addie finally sat down in the parlour beside Jake. She wore a long formal dress but had casually covered her shoulders with her new cashmere cardigan. Jake's sweater was visible under his dark suit. Tretheway sat across the room resplendent in his new smoking jacket. O. Pitts could be heard moving glasses around in the kitchen.

"I think everything's done," Addie sighed.

Tretheway and Jake had laboured for more than an hour before dinner. They had rolled up some of the rugs, moved the Christmas tree into a corner away from the open fireplace and shovelled snow from the verandah and front sidewalk. But Addie had worked hard all day. Small, dainty sandwiches were piled on numerous serving trays. Ice cubes, borrowed from neighbours, filled the ice-box. Soft drinks, a case of soda siphons and forty-eight quarts of Molson Blue were cooling on the back porch. The floors gleamed where they showed around the scatter rugs, except in the sun-room where talcum powder had been spread for dancing. Paper hats, horns and other noisemakers were at the ready in the kitchen. A traditional ham warmed in the oven; fresh bread, cookies and heavy cakes filled the pantry.

"I can't do anything else, anyway," Addie said. "It's too late."

The doorbell rang. Tretheway and Jake stood up while Addie left the parlour to answer the door.

"Hello, Sergeant," they heard her say. "Gentlemen. Step in out of the cold."

"Addie," Wan Ho acknowledged. "Are we the first?"

"Somebody has to be."

Tretheway and Jake went to the front door to greet Wan Ho and the three plainclothesmen who were there, if anybody asked, to mix and serve drinks. During the hellos and discarding of coats, the doorbell ran again.

"Jake," Tretheway suggested, "why don't you show the boys where everything is? Liquor, glasses, ice cubes." He lowered his voice. "Doors, windows, general layout." His voice returned to normal. "I'll get the door."

"Right." Jake led the first four arrivals to the kitchen.

When Tretheway opened the front door, his shadow fell across the smiling face of Bartholomew Gum and what he first thought were four RCMP officers on the verandah behind the Alderman.

"Bartholomew?" Tretheway questioned.

"Evening, Inspector." Gum turned to the group behind him.

"Boys, this is Inspector Tretheway." They gave Tretheway a smart Scout salute.

"Isn't that nice," Addie said from behind Tretheway. "Ask them in, Albert."

Tretheway stepped out of the way and looked a question at Addie.

"Bartholomew thought it'd be nice if the boys could serve sandwiches and things. And so did I. His mother couldn't come," she explained.

"We certainly have enough help now," Tretheway said, still smiling. He missed the look that passed over Addie's face. "This way, boys."

Emmett O'Dell arrived next. A Scout, who appeared suddenly at his side, peeled the Alderman's coat from his back to reveal a new, bright green blazer that he had given himself for Christmas.

"What a pretty coat," Addie said.

"Thank you." Emmett O'Dell smiled. "It was a present."

For the next fifteen minutes, there was a steady stream of guests.

The most conspicuous entrance was made by Joseph Pennylegion, or really, the Pennylegion party. From out of the two long sleek black sedans parked at the foot of the Tretheways' sidewalk, Controller Pennylegion led his group up the verandah steps and through the door.

"Miss Tretheway." He bowed and doffed his white beaver hat. His dark grey coat, trimmed with Persian lamb and lined with shimmering scarlet satin, was draped over his shoulders like a cape.

"Controller Pennylegion." Addie looked over his head at the others.

The present Mrs Pennylegion (his second) was right behind her husband (her first). She was much younger then he with hair the same flaming red as his. Her too-tight fuschia evening gown made walking difficult. The four others—aides, bodyguards, or as Tretheway called them, the tasters—nodded silently at Addie as they passed. They wore tuxedos, while Controller Pennylegion sported a fashionable white dinner jacket.

"Thought maybe they could change records or something," Pennylegion said.

"Oh, dear," Addie said, but she smiled.

Morgan Morgan and Gertrude Valentini arrived at the same

time, although not together. With his regimental tie and the miniature medals that he was entitled to wear on formal occasions, Morgan looked every bit the successful military campaigner, even in mufti.

Mrs Valentini wore a long dress she had cut and sewn herself in which she still looked motherly, but festive. It was red, white and green with ruffles. She carried a bulky matching purse.

"Don't you look Christmasy," Addie remarked.

Tretheway thought she also resembled the Italian flag. He left the hall area to ease the congestion and, at the same time, to check on the party. Soon after, Mac arrived with his four Sea Scouts.

Tretheway knew about Wan Ho's extra men and Gum's Scouts. The Pennylegion helpers were a surprise. And Addie had simply forgotten to tell her brother about accepting Mac's kind offer of extra help.

"Here we are, Addie." Mac led his patrol in. "Where do you want the boys?"

"Oh, dear," Addie said again, but she didn't smile.

Tretheway pushed his way back through the new arrivals. He motioned Addie over. "Who are they?" he asked.

"They're Mac's Scouts," Addie explained. "They're going to help."

"Addie, we've got more helpers than guests."

"They can take coats. And open doors."

The doorbell rang. One of Mac's Scouts opened it immediately.

"See?" Addie ducked around Tretheway toward the door.

The Zulps' entrance was spoiled by the coincidental arrival of Fred, the Labrador.

"Evening, Tretheway," Zulp rasped.

"Hello, Inspector." Mrs Zulp's voice was quiet and melodious, in direct contrast to her husband's. "Have a good Christmas?"

"Very enjoyable, Mrs Zulp."

"New jacket?"

"From Addie."

"Nice."

"Lots of wear left in this one." Zulp brushed some lint from his shiny blue serge lapel.

Tretheway noticed one of Mac's Scouts jostling with one of Gum's Scouts for the privilege of hanging up the Zulps' coats.

"Don't make 'em like they used to," Zulp went on. He waved down the hall to several people who hadn't yet made it to the party room or kitchen. Before any of them could wave back, Fred bounded in the open door. For the next five minutes, everyone made a fuss over the dog while Zulp stood by uncomfortably.

When Dr Nooner came in, he made straight for Tretheway.

"I trust I won't be needed professionally tonight." Nooner exhibited a black sense of humour after a few drinks. "I didn't even bring my bag."

"Just as well," Tretheway said, turning his head away from the fumes.

"Dance started?" Nooner shouldered his way down the hall before Tretheway could answer.

"You look good in red, Tretheway," was Mayor Trutt's greeting. "Makes you look smaller."

Tretheway grunted and nodded at Mrs Trutt.

Mayor Trutt smacked his hands together gleefully. "I do like a party." He extended his arm to Mrs Trutt. "Shall we join the others?"

His wife nodded and smiled politely in answer to her husband's request, as she usually did. They followed Dr Nooner down the hall.

As each new arrival entered the sunroom, he or she added his or her bit to the noise level. The hum of conversation, plus the music from the central P.A. system and the clinking of glasses, rose to normal party volume which increased as the celebration pressed onward. No one was left with an empty glass for more than a few seconds. At times, two Scouts, one of Gum's and one of Mac's, would arrive at the same time, in front of the same guest, with a fresh drink. Tretheway noticed that the competition between the two groups seemed more than just a healthy inter-Scout rivalry.

With all this activity, it was just as well that Pennylegion's four had decided, or were told, to stay close to home and wait only on their employer. Most of the other guests moved about and socialized. There were small groups forming and dispersing constantly; nothing lasted. Or, as Tretheway said to Jake, he couldn't see any pattern yet.

"And maybe nothing will happen," Tretheway confided to Jake. They were both in the kitchen. Tretheway had just wrestled a large pail of ice cubes in from the back porch. He handed it to Jake.

"If anything does happen," Jake started, "ah . . . just when . . ."

"Twelve o'clock."

Jake dropped the bucket. Some ice spilled onto the floor. "Midnight?"

Tretheway lifted the bucket again. "Now pick the ice up."

"Wan Ho needs some more ice," O. Pitts shouted from the doorway.

Tretheway handed the bucket back to Jake. "Take this in."

"But . . ." Jake protested.

"I can't tell you any more." Tretheway glanced over Jake's shoulder at the inquisitive face of O. Pitts. "Just keep your eyes open." He went back to the porch for some cold beer and pop.

When Jake carried the ice into the sunroom, Addie caught his eye. Jake smiled a reassurance at her that he didn't feel and kept walking.

"Need ice?" he asked Wan Ho unnecessarily.

"Thank you." Wan Ho accepted the ice.

"Everything okay?"

Wan Ho shrugged. "How about you?"

"Nothing funny yet," Jake said.

They listened to the music. Kay Kayser's rendition of "South of the Border" reverberated across the room. Several couples were dancing.

"Tretheway says midnight," Jake said.

"Does he know what will happen?" Wan Ho asked.

It was Jake's turn to shrug. Tretheway arrived with the cold beer and pop.

For the next couple of hours, Tretheway mixed with his guests, but curbed his drinking and watched. The only really suspicious-looking activity he saw was being carried on by Jake, Wan Ho and the three plainclothesmen who were doing the same thing he was. He decided that dancing would make him less conspicuous. For his first partner, he selected Gertrude Valentini. Short enough, he reasoned, to give him an unobstructed view of everyone.

Tretheway danced confidently. As Addie said, with her own particular logic, "Albert looks so much thinner when he dances." But tonight, he gave little thought to his appearance.

As he fox-trotted Mrs Valentini around the floor and automatically answered her small talk, Tretheway watched for some behaviour that would confirm or reject his suspicions. He watched for something to happen. Which meant, he watched everything.

The Pennylegion bunch broke up. Two of the hirelings went to the bar, the third followed his boss to the downstairs toilet while the fourth, Quick Roy, danced with a bored Mrs Pennylegion. Addie carried empty sandwich plates into the kitchen. Dr Nooner explained his new golf swing theory to Jake while O. Pitts pretended to understand. Mayor Trutt and his Missus joined the bachelor twosome of Morgan Morgan and MacCulla, effectively stopping Morgan in the middle of an off-colour story. Emmett O'Dell stood by himself sipping Irish whiskey. He was very close to singing. Mr and Mrs Zulp sat beside the fireplace waiting for someone to visit with them. He was drinking scotch neat. The two sets of Scouts weaved their tortuous paths and plied the guests with food and drink, although Tretheway found it hard to keep track of them. Bartholomew Gum was searching for a dancing partner. Mrs O'Dell was nowhere to be seen.

Tretheway saw all this in the time it took one record to finish— approximately three minutes. And every three minutes the record, and a certain number of people, changed. Frankie Carle replaced Kay Kayser. Bridget O'Dell came back into the room ostensibly from the upstairs bathroom. Morgan Morgan took his story and looked for another group. Joseph Pennylegion returned and danced with his wife. She still looked bored. O. Pitts disappeared.

Tretheway soon realized that it was impossible to tell where everybody was at all times. He hoped his surveillance would dovetail, rather than overlap, with Jake's and Wan Ho's. Also, he consoled himself, the killer had to think he had a certain amount of freedom or he wouldn't show himself.

"Have you any idea what a rutabaga costs nowadays?"

"What?" Tretheway looked down, surprised.

"And they're not easy to find, either," Gertrude Valentini continued.

Tretheway had forgotten Mrs Valentini. "What's not easy to find?"

"Rutabagas." She didn't seem to notice Tretheway's inattention. "It's the War."

"I see." Tretheway wondered what she had been saying while the last two records had played. The music stopped.

"I'll ask Addie," she said. "She knows all about food."

Tretheway watched the diminutive red, white and green figure of Mrs Valentini head toward the kitchen—unsteadily, he thought.

At eleven-thirty, Tretheway caught Jake and Wan Ho alone at the bar. "Anything?" he asked.

"Nothing," Jake said.

Wan Ho shook his head. "Everyone leaves the room at one time or another. But nothing suspicious."

"Did you check outside?" Tretheway persisted.

"Yes." Jake flipped another peanut at Fred the Labrador. "Me and Fred. Nothing's amiss."

"What about . . .?" Wan Ho cocked his head at Zulp across the room. He was still sitting in the same spot, his chair tipped back precariously against the wall. Mrs Zulp was no longer beside him. The heat from the fireplace had reddened Zulp's face and wrinkled his collar. And his eyes were becoming glazed from the perpetual stream of Scout-delivered scotches.

"I don't think we should bother him," Tretheway said. "He looks content."

"I'll bet he's even forgotten about Gilbert and Sullivan," Jake chuckled.

A Scout pulled at Tretheway's sleeve.

"Nothing for me, son." Tretheway thumped his fist on the bar. "Dammit, Jake. Something's got to happen."

The Scout pulled again. Tretheway looked down to see one of Gum's Scouts standing in front of him with his arm outstretched. The boy's upturned palm held a small, wet object.

"I said no, thank you."

"It's my tooth." The Scout lisped when his tongue hit the unfamiliar space between his teeth.

"Eh?"

"My tooth. Someone knocked out my tooth. In the cellar." The Scout was close to tears.

Tretheway blinked. "Who did it?"

"I couldn't see. Too dark. My mouth hurts."

"Take it easy now." Tretheway looked at Jake. "Any pop?"

Wan Ho poured a cold glass of KIK and handed it to the Scout. It settled him down.

"Now what happened?" Tretheway asked.

"I went downstairs to the toilet. Then I heard this noise. Then I saw this guy in the corner. Bending down. Fooling around with the big thing downstairs."

"What big thing?" Tretheway asked.

"I don't know. You got it all covered up."

"The Machine." Jake looked at Tretheway.

"Go on." Tretheway encouraged the Scout.

"Then I went over to the corner. Then I said, 'What are you doing?' Then he hit me in the mouth." The Scout pushed his little finger experimentally through the hole in his teeth.

"And you don't know who it was?" Tretheway asked.

The Scout shook his head. "No. I guess I fell. Then I felt dizzy. Then I saw stars. And when I opened my eyes, no one was there." He held his empty glass out for a refill.

Tretheway surveyed the festivities. No one appeared to be watching them. Pennylegion was alone. His wife and men were not in sight. Only one of the Sea Scouts was in view. Gertrude Valentini was missing and Tretheway couldn't spot Emmett O'Dell.

"Watch the door, Jake. Don't let anyone down." Tretheway started for the stairs.

"But how . . ." Jake began.

"Tell them the toilet's plugged."

Tretheway walked across the room as nonchalantly as he could. He nodded routinely to Bartholomew Gum who was now dancing with Mrs Trutt. Tretheway entered the inner hall and started down the stairs. The only furtive individual he saw through the crack in the closing door was Jake coming over to stand guard.

Tretheway bounded nimbly down the steps. He walked around the furnace, past the coal bin to the place he figured the young Scout had been talking about. There was a light at the top of the stairs but it was dark enough here, Tretheway reasoned, so that you might not recognize an assailant. He reached up and pulled the overhead chain. Light flooded into the uneven pools of dark grey on the lumpy tarpaulin that covered The Machine. He walked around the structure, inspecting, while his eyes became accustomed to the harsh light.

At first, everything appeared to be in its place. Then at the lower end of The Machine, Tretheway spotted fresh creases in the dust, as though the cover had recently been carefully folded back and, just as carefully, replaced. He grabbed the corner of the tarp. With a cautionary sixth sense he had developed over the years as a successful policeman, Tretheway gently lifted the covering.

Locked in the business end of The Machine, where Addie's milk and Morgan's whiskey had been weeks before, was a glass vial about the size of an upright frankfurter. It contained what looked like plain water. And it was corked.

Tretheway stared at it, outwardly calm, while unsettling questions and answers bounced around inside his head. He finally squatted down and tried, very carefully, to remove the cork. It came out easily. There was a slippery, oily feel to it. On impulse, Tretheway touched the wet end of the cork to his tongue. He experienced a sweet burning taste and an instant headache.

"Jezuz!" He replaced the cork even more carefully. Still squatting, Tretheway tried to remember the chemistry books he had researched in preparation for tonight—one phrase in particular. He concentrated. A final shot of adrenalin pumped out the elusive sentence as clearly as if a chemistry teacher had chalked it on the blackboard. "To prevent an explosion, the ester must be decomposed by the addition of alkali."

Tretheway stood up quickly. "Valentini!" He slapped his thigh. "Gertrude Valentini!"

When he pushed open the door at the top of the cellar stairs, Tretheway knocked a startled Jake into the potted plant that stood across the small inner hall.

"Valentini's purse," Tretheway said without explanation.

"Eh?" Jake brushed a fern leaf from his shoulder.

Tretheway forced himself to speak slowly, while still imparting urgency to his order. "Alderman Gertrude Valentini. Bring me her purse."

"But how . . ."

"Steal the goddam thing!" Tretheway forced himself once again to speak calmly. "Bring it downstairs. Get Wan Ho to replace you on the door. Don't let anyone see you. And hurry."

Jake stared at the door after it closed and listened to Tretheway's descending footsteps. "Mrs Valentini's purse," he said resignedly out loud to himself.

Jake pushed his way through the dancers. Addie saw him and tried to get his attention. He pretended not to notice and pushed on. In his hurried search for Mrs Valentini, Jake absently noted a few changes. The O'Dells were two-stepping to a Paul White-man waltz. Zulp was still participating but had slipped lower in his chair. Morgan Morgan was telling a story to the Pennylegion men. Mrs Pennylegion was listening and, for the first time, didn't look bored. When Jake found Mrs Valentini, she was discussing the Italian flag with O. Pitts.

"It was originally the banner of Napoleon's Italian Legion," O. Pitts was saying. "The 1796 campaign."

"My, my," Mrs Valentini replied.

"He designed it."

"Who?"

"Napoleon. The Italian flag."

"Oh."

"That's why it looks so much like the French flag."

"I see." Mrs Valentini looked puzzled.

Jake noticed the purse by itself on a small low table in full view of the two conversationalists. He was racking his brains for ways to divert their attention when Emmett O'Dell came to his rescue. The Irish Alderman belted unannounced into the chorus of "Mrs Murphy's Chowder", easily drowning out Paul Whiteman. Every eye in the room went to him, including Mrs Valentini's and O. Pitts'. Before Mrs O'Dell could quiet down her husband, Jake stuffed the bulky red, white and green evening bag up his cash-mere sweater. He left unnoticed, he thought, and made for the bar feeling reasonably pleased with the first part of his mission.

"Why did you steal Mrs Valentini's purse?" Wan Ho asked.

"You saw?" Jake said.

Wan Ho nodded professionally.

"Did anybody else see?" Jake asked.

"I don't think so. But why?"

"I was ordered to," Jake explained. "I have to take it down to the cellar to the Inspector. He wants you to take my place at the door."

"What's going on?"

"You now know as much as I do."

Jake pushed his way back toward the inner hall. He had to pass between Emmett O'Dell, now seated, and Mrs O'Dell, who was consoling him. "Wait till after 'Auld Lang Syne'," Jake heard her say.

When Jake arrived at Tretheway's side, the purse had already slipped halfway out of his sweater. Tretheway grabbed it just before it fell to the floor. He opened it roughly and, without compunction, dumped the contents onto a low bench beside The Machine. A set of keys, three floral scented handkerchiefs, a letter, two dark lipsticks, newspaper clippings about the Atlantic sea war, a pencil stub, two eight-ounce unlabelled full bottles, one eight ounce unlabelled empty bottle, paper clips and, naturally, some smelling salts, were among the unsuspicious objects.

"There it is," Tretheway announced.

Jake picked up the empty bottle. "This?" He unscrewed the top and sniffed. "Smells like turnips."

"No." Tretheway picked up the smaller bottle. "This one."

"Smelling salts?" Jake asked.

"Anyone that faints that much has to have smelling salts." Tretheway took the top off. A heady aroma filled the air. "Ammonia," he said.

"What?"

"An alkali."

Tretheway squatted down beside The Machine. Jake squatted also. Tretheway pointed. "You see that cork?"

Jake nodded.

"Take it out. Very carefully. Under no circumstances make a sudden move."

"Should I ask why?"

"No."

Jake steadied himself and did as he was told. When the cork came out, a faint sweet smell mingled with the ammonia already in the air.

"Good boy." Tretheway touched the jar of Mrs Valentini's smelling salts to the open neck of the vial. He tipped it slowly until the ammonia ran down the inside of the vial and mixed with the colourless liquid. Some of the camphor lumps fell into the solution. There was a sudden bubbling reaction.

"It's boiling," Jake said.

"Exothermic reaction," Tretheway said.

"What?"

"Didn't you learn that at FYU?"

"I took history."

The two watched while the liquid settled. It appeared unchanged. "Good," Tretheway said.

"What did we just do?" Jake asked.

"Decomposed an ester. Put the cover back the way it was."

Jake reached out for the tarp.

"Gently," Tretheway said.

"We still have to be careful?"

"Let's say extra safe."

"But I thought we just . . ."

"I'm a policeman. Not a goddam chemist."

When the cover was safely in place, Tretheway walked away. Jake replaced Mrs Valentini's belongings in her purse and followed. He stopped just in time to avoid a collision when Tretheway halted abruptly at the foot of the cellar stairs. Tretheway turned around. "What's the time?"

Jake checked his wrist. "Eleven-thirty."

"And how long does The Machine take to smash a bottle?"

"Ten minutes."

"That gives us twenty minutes." Tretheway searched fruitlessly in his new pockets for a cigar. "Let's go look for someone with a tooth mark on his hand. Presumably his right hand."

"Right," Jake said.

"And get rid of that purse."

When Jake successfully sneaked the purse back onto the table he had taken it from, it gave him a chance to check the hands of Mrs Valentini and O. Pitts. They were clean. While Jake chose simply to look, Tretheway's method was to shake hands. But he too found nothing. From the limp fishy handshake of Controller MacCulla to the surprisingly strong grip of Mayor Trutt, Tretheway found no cuts, bruises or tooth marks.

They met back at the bar. One of Wan Ho's men handed them each a beer. Wan Ho was still guarding the cellar door.

"Nothing?" Tretheway asked Jake.

Jake shook his head.

"Are you sure?"

Jake nodded.

"You checked everybody?"

Jake nodded again.

Tretheway took a long pull of Molson Blue. He surveyed the dance floor. Gum's Scouts were still efficiently serving drinks and sandwiches.

"The Scouts," Tretheway said.

Jake swallowed fast. "Eh?"

"Did you check the Scouts?"

Jake followed Tretheway's gaze. "They wouldn't punch one of their own."

"Did you check Mac's Scouts?"

"No." Jake looked around the room. "I can't see them."

"I can't see Mac, either." Tretheway pushed his way across the room with Jake in his wake. They nodded and smiled their way past the guests until they reached Addie.

"Everything all right?" she asked them in a tone that begged for a happy, even if untrue, answer.

"Have you seen Mac?" Tretheway ignored her question.

"Why, yes." Addie pointed. "He went into the kitchen a few minutes ago."

Tretheway made for the kitchen.

"Everything's fine, Addie." Jake patted her arm and felt the soft texture of his gift. "Don't you worry."

Addie smiled an answer.

When Jake pushed through the swinging door of the kitchen, he found Tretheway standing in the centre of the empty room.

"Where is he?" Jake asked.

"Has to be outside." Tretheway went to the back door. He stepped out onto the porch. Jake followed. Tretheway didn't notice the cold.

"Maybe we should get our coats on." Jake shivered.

"No time."

"But it's still snowing."

"Good." Tretheway pointed to a set of fresh footprints leading away from the porch. "There's our man."

Once off the shovelled porch they became part of the winter night. The wind howled about their bare heads, at times stinging their cheeks and eyes with snowflakes. They followed the trail, crouching like common burglars, with Jake trying to place his street shoes into the larger holes in the snow made by Tretheway's boots. As they rounded the corner of the old house, a large black flying object hit Tretheway square in the chest. He fell back on Jake with the black thing on top of both of them. Tretheway swung wildly. He felt a sudden swoosh of hot breath on his face as his fist sunk into the soft belly of Fred the Labrador. The dog yelped. She jumped off Tretheway's chest.

"Damdog!" Tretheway scrambled to his feet and pulled Jake up. "Why'd he do that?"

"It's the snow."

"Eh?"

"She goes funny when it's fresh. Didn't mean anything. Just playful. Here, Fred." The dog, wheezing sheepishly, came to Jake. "Good girl." He rubbed her stomach.

"What the hell are you petting him for?"

"She thinks she did something bad."

"He did!"

Jake didn't answer.

"Keep him quiet." Tretheway started on the trail again.

It led them along the back of the house. They could hear enough of the party sounds through the thick walls of the sunroom to know that Addie had tuned in Guy Lombardo and Times Square. Tretheway stopped at the forsythia hedge, now weighed down with snow, which separated this part of the garden from the driveway.

"The garage." Tretheway spread some of the branches apart with his bare hands and peered through. "I think it goes to the garage."

"Can you see anything?" Jake tried to see through the hedge.

"We'll have to get closer. I can't . . . wait a minute."

"What?"

"Someone's there."

"Where?" Jake whispered.

Tretheway pointed.

They watched through the falling flakes while a shadowy figure left the black square of the open garage door and flitted from bush to evergreen in its progress down the driveway. As the figure left the protection of a large elm tree, the capricious wind swirled the snow away from their line of sight. For a short but clear second, they saw their quarry silhouetted against a snowbank before it disappeared around the side of the house.

"You see that?" Tretheway asked.

"Yes." Jake nodded excitedly. "Looked like some sort of uniform. And a funny hat."

"Not a hat. A pickelhaube."

"What?"

"A broken pickelhaube."

A clanging sound of metal against metal interrupted their discussion. For the second time since he had left the house, Jake felt a chill.

"Let's go." Tretheway stepped out from behind the forsythia and bulldozed his way through a drift with, Jake thought, nowhere near enough caution. And Jake could think of no good reason not to follow. Halfway down, Tretheway stopped. "Look." He pointed at the ground. Other footprints joined the ones they were following to create a confusing pattern.

"Where'd they go?" Jake asked.

Tretheway looked up and down the empty driveway.

"Up the wall?" Jake suggested.

Tretheway shook his head.

"Did they double back?"

"We'd've seen them."

"Around the front?"

"Didn't have time."

"They can't just disappear."

In a three foot section of jog, a square iron door faced the street for the convenience of coal delivery. Tretheway pointed. "The coal chute!" He lifted the heavy cast-iron door and propped it open. The opening and beyond was black. Nothing could be seen. The two of them squatted down and listened.

Sounds overlapped. They heard the wind in the distance; they heard the spinning wheels of a nearby car stuck in the snow; they heard the muffled sounds of Guy Lombardo; they heard Fred panting; but most distinctly of all, they heard someone shouting in a language they didn't understand.

"Give me your revolver," Tretheway said to Jake.

"I don't have it."

"Where is it?"

"At the office."

"Damn!"

"What about yours?"

"We'll have to go in without them."

"Don't you think we should tell someone? Like Wan Ho? Or his men? I'll bet they've got guns."

Tretheway ignored Jake's questions. "I'll go first." He stood up and made another quick decision. "Feet first."

With Jake helping, Tretheway climbed into the opening as quietly as possible. It was adequate for most of his body. His feet, legs and lower parts slid smoothly down the metallic chute with no problem. Then, with his arms pinned to his sides and only his head and shoulders protruding from the hole in the wall, what Jake knew was bound to happen, happened.

"I can't go any further," Tretheway said.

"Eh?"

"Push!"

Jake pushed as hard as he could.

"It's no good," Tretheway said. "Pull me out. I'll try head first."

Jake exerted himself in the other direction.

"Harder!"

He pulled harder and still Tretheway didn't budge. Jake straightened up, breathing heavily. Fred licked Tretheway's face.

"Do something!"

Jake leaned over close to Tretheway's head, which now appeared upside down to him. "This might hurt a little, but it's our only chance."

"Hurry up!"

Jake ran back across the driveway and up a large snow bank. He turned and faced Tretheway. Rocking back and forth on his feet like a decathlon champion at the start of a high jump run, Jake readied himself for the attempt. The back door opened.

"Albert! Are you out there?" Addie shouted. "It's almost midnight. Jake!"

Jake took off down the snow bank and across the driveway. He leaped high in the air just before he got to Tretheway. His jump was perfectly timed. With his legs straight out ahead of him, knees locked, he landed with his full hundred and forty pounds astride Tretheway's head, one foot on each shoulder. The force was enough to pop Tretheway loose. He disappeared down the chute.

Jake lay in the snow and listened. Tretheway's bellow echoed from the depths of the cellar. Whether it was caused by pain, fear, rage, or was simply a battle cry, Jake could only guess. He scrambled to his knees and poked his head into the opening. Black dust stung his eyes and offended his nostrils. He heard the sounds of coal shifting noisily with lumps hitting the wooden sides of the bin. A poker clanged on the concrete floor. Someone cursed in German. Then, except for the party noises upstairs, there was silence.

"You okay?" Jake shouted down the chute.

"Come down," Tretheway answered.

"I'll take the stairs."

"Now!"

Jake shook his head and thought about the teaching job he had passed up to join the force. He pulled his jacket tightly around him to protect his new sweater. Closing his eyes, he pushed off with his legs and slid head first into the coal bin. His alarmingly fast slide down the chute, worn smooth with years of coal delivery, stopped abruptly when his head hit the shock-absorbing mound of Tretheway's stomach.

Jake picked himself up. "Sorry, Boss." He trod unsteadily on the lumps of coal at the edge of the pile. "Let me help you up."

Tretheway, temporarily out of breath, didn't answer. With Jake's help he turned over, got to his knees and finally regained his feet.

"Are you all right?" Jake flicked coal dust from Tretheway's new smoking jacket and his own suit.

"Never mind that now." Tretheway pointed over Jake's shoulder. Jake turned around.

Five shadowy figures, dramatically backlit by the single overhead bulb, crouched threateningly in a defensive half-circle around The Machine. The chromium ball swung rhythmically from the miniature tower already three-quarters of the way down the ramp. A brilliant highlight shimmered on the vial locked in the lower end of The Machine. And five shadowy arms each held a handgun.

"God," Jake said softly.

Four of the five were small calibre revolvers. They wavered slightly, but pointed at Tretheway and Jake. The fifth, an ugly automatic Mauser pistol, flailed wildly through the air in the white-gloved hand of . . . Tretheway wasn't sure.

"You have two minutes to live!" the figure shouted.

Tretheway didn't recognize the voice, the B-movie German accent, nor the uniform, or really, the costume . . .

A broad red stripe ran down the grey legs of the trousers; one leg was tucked in, one leg hung over the scruffy, knee-high riding boots. The navy blue tunic with a scarlet high-necked collar and matching cuffs supported a pair of oversized gold epaulets with matching embroidery. Decorations glittered on the figure's chest. A dull gun-metal grey Iron Cross hung at his throat. This Tretheway did recognize. And a broken pickelhaube, slightly askew and throwing the face into deep shadow, capped this apparition of nineteenth century Prussian military might. The figure raised his head to the light.

"In one and one half minutes we all die for the Fatherland!"

Despite the dark coal smudges on his features, both Tretheway and Jake recognized MacCulla.

Tretheway noticed a change of expression come over the other four—Mac's Sea Scouts. In the cellar light, their navy uniforms appeared black. Homemade white crossbelts formed x's on the four young chests. One Scout, slightly taller than the others, wore silver epaulets, the mark of an NCO. And four genuine pickelhaubes, chinstrapped into position, glistened menacingly. Tretheway recalled the pointed heads he first saw at the top of the paper pile the night Henry Plain suffocated. Three of the Scouts lowered their 22s and looked at their leader. The tall NCO kept his revolver trained on Tretheway and Jake, but also looked a question at MacCulla. Mac ignored them. It appeared to Tretheway that, as far as the Scouts were concerned, being part of the explosion was not part of the plan.

"Sir," the NCO Scout began, "you said . . ."

"Courage above all things is the first quality of a warrior!" Mac shouted.

Tretheway could see that The Machine was less than two minutes away from its climax. And the Scouts knew it. He wasn't so sure about MacCulla.

"Stay full of good courage!" Mac's eyes were large. Drool wet his chin. "Fight with zeal and spirit!"

Tretheway took one calculated pace toward The Machine. The NCO Scout pointed his revolver at Tretheway's stomach.

"Do you know what's in that vial?" Tretheway transfixed one of the other Scouts with a glare that had bent stronger people to his will.

"Ni . . . Ni . . ." the Scout stammered.

"Nitroglycerin," the other two answered together.

"There's enough there to blow up the whole house." Tretheway stabbed his coal-stained finger at the Scouts. "And you along with it!" He thought he saw even the NCO Scout's lip tremble.

"A commander must show great energy of purpose!" MacCulla ranted on, paying them little attention.

Tretheway heard a commotion at the head of the stairs. Addie was trying to get by Wan Ho. The door opened.

"Albert! Jake!" Addie shouted. "Are you down there? It's one minute to twelve o'clock!"

Tretheway sensed Jake's sudden tension. So did the NCO Scout. His revolver swung around. Jake lunged forward. With the speed of a snake's tongue, Tretheway's arm shot out. Jake's progress was stopped when Tretheway's ample hand grabbed him by the neck. He pulled Jake back and turned him around. Their eyes were inches apart.

"Have faith." Tretheway watched the fear and courage in Jake's eyes give way to perplexed trust.

"I know you're down there," Addie shouted.

The noise of the party intruded through the open door. Premature experimental toots on horns sounded in anticipation of midnight. The radio blared. Someone started counting the seconds.

"Ten! Nine! Eight!"

The Machine hummed on.

"The field of genius raises itself above the rules!" MacCulla raved.

"Seven! Six!"

At five, the three Scouts dropped their revolvers. One ripped off his pickelhaube and sank weeping to his knees. The other two bolted for the coal bin.

"I'm coming down!" Addie shouted.

"Three! Two!"

"Decision by arms!" MacCulla screamed.

At midnight, several things happened at once. The swinging metal ball smashed full into the vial, spattering the harmless liquid around the room. Tretheway let go of Jake, stepped forward and took the gun from the remaining NCO Scout with no fuss. Jake grabbed the two escaping Scouts. Fred came down the coal chute. The upstairs revellers swung noisemakers, blew horns, threw streams of paper and cheered. Mac raised his gun hand and fired his unbelieveably loud Mauser pistol, sending a bullet through the rafters, through the hardwood floor of the sun room, through one of Addie's Persian rugs, through the seat of Zulp's chair and slightly penetrated the fleshy part of the Chief's right buttock. Guy Lombardo struck up "Auld Lang Syne".

JANUARY, 1941

In January, 1941, the German city of Bremen was bombed with incendiaries for three and a half hours in retaliation for the fire raids on London; Stanford defeated Nebraska in the Rose Bowl; a local movie house screened the musical *Tin Pan Alley* starring Alice Faye and Jack Oakie; Bette Davis married someone called Arthur Farnsworth; Eli Culbertson explained a five diamond bid; the Toronto Maple Leafs stayed in first place, a skating step ahead of the Detroit Red Wings; and an alarming sequence of events took place on New Year's Eve at the home of Inspector Tretheway.

All these events were reported in the first *Fort York Expositor* of the year, published and delivered on the second of January, a Thursday. The last item filled the front page of the second section.

It began:

At the stroke of midnight, festivities came to a shuddering halt when Chief Horace Zulp was felled by a madman's bullet while attending a New Year's Eve celebration at the Tretheway residence. During the melee, the infamous Holiday Killer was unmasked. Who? None other than Controller (Mac) MacCulla. Inspector A. V. Tretheway, Constable Jonathan Small and Sergeant of Detectives Wan Ho also took part in the arrest.

Near a large picture of the Chief, the item went on to say, among other things, that Zulp was out of danger and would be back at his desk fighting the enemies of society again in a few days. The story contained many mistakes.

Zulp *was* out of danger, but then, he was never *in* danger. He *was* gunned down, but nobody realized it. When the bullet partially entered his rear, there was still enough force from the powerful projectile to knock the chair down along with Zulp. He was immediately replaced in his uprighted seat by two Boy Scouts and continued to enjoy the party.

Hours later Mrs Zulp noticed the large bruise on her husband's

170

backside when they were undressing for bed. What little blood there was had been absorbed by his clothing. And when Mrs Zulp plucked the squashed bullet from her husband's rear and examined it, she concluded that it was probably a misshapen upholstery tack from Addie's dining room chair. One of Wan Ho's men actually traced the bullet's path and correctly deduced what had happened. Zulp was far from the first one to know he had been shot.

And the festivities did not come to an abrupt halt. Most of the guests partied on into the wee hours and went home, like the Zulps, not realizing what had happened. In all the commotion at midnight, few people guessed it was a shot when MacCulla squeezed off his last round. Those in the cellar, of course, knew.

After Tretheway had carefully pried the Mauser from Mac-Culla's clenched fist, Jake explained things to Addie. She punctuated his explanation with tongue clucks and several "Oh, dears" while absently brushing coal dust from his sweater. But she took the frightening events well.

"I'd better look after our other guests," Addie said finally. She turned and started back up the stairs.

"Would you send my men down, Addie?" Wan Ho had followed Addie downstairs.

"And Doc Nooner," Tretheway added with his eye on MacCulla.

MacCulla had stood quietly all this time. He appeared stunned, alternately smiling and frowning. And always averting his eyes from his Scouts. Tretheway approached him. He placed his hand gently on Mac's shoulder. Mac jumped.

"Why?" Tretheway asked.

"Wh . . . what?" MacCulla successfully focused his gaze on Tretheway. His pickelhaube was pushed to the back of his head. He rubbed at his eyes and further dirtied his coal-streaked face. His collar was undone. An epaulet had fallen off.

"All those people," Tretheway went on. "Taz, Father Cosentino, Miss Tommerup. And the others. Why did you do it?"

"Politics."

"What?"

"You guys have a coal fight?" Dr Nooner appeared beside Tretheway.

"The conduct of war is political policy," MacCulla said.

"What's he talking about?" Nooner asked.

"It takes up the sword instead of the pen."

"Would you mind checking him over?" Tretheway pointed at Mac.

"Why?" Nooner questioned.

"We must burn with a passionate hatred of one another!" Mac shouted.

"Because I'm taking him to jail," Tretheway said.

"Jail?" Nooner questioned again.

"He's the killer!"

"All right." Nooner seemed more sober than before. "I'll talk to him."

"Mac!" Mac blinked, but seemed to focus on Tretheway. "I want you to talk to Doc Nooner."

"I talk to the others," Mac said.

"What others?" Nooner asked.

"Clausewitz?" Jake suggested.

"No, no," Mac said. "Don't be silly."

"That's something," Nooner sighed.

"I *am* Clausewitz."

Tretheway and Nooner exchanged looks.

"I talk to Marie."

"Marie?" Nooner repeated.

"Mrs Clausewitz," Mac said impatiently. "And sometimes to Scharnhorst. And King Frederick the Third. Or was it the Second?"

"That's okay, Mac," Tretheway said. "Take it easy."

"And Machiavelli. Now there was a . . ." Mac's voice dwindled off. He stared around the room. Everyone was watching him. He offered no resistance when Wan Ho handcuffed him.

It was ascertained that MacCulla was physically all right. He had just lapsed into silence. As Dr Nooner said, raising an eyebrow at Tretheway, "He's just reacting to whatever happened down here." Nooner also said that MacCulla was healthy enough to go to jail but, if possible, could questioning be postponed until tomorrow?

Tretheway nodded. "Unless he volunteers anything."

Dr Nooner nodded.

Tretheway planned the logistics.

"Jake, you lead the way. Then two Scouts. Then you." Tretheway pointed at Wan Ho's men. "Then the other two Scouts. Wan Ho. Nooner. MacCulla and I'll bring up the rear. Let's go. Right to the cars."

"Do we have to go up where everybody can see us?" Jake asked.

"You want to go up the coal chute?"

Jake started up the stairs without answering. In his excitement he led the file of men from the inner hall through the sunroom instead of unobtrusively out the back door as Tretheway had assumed he would. And by the time Tretheway got there, it was too late to change direction.

The merry-making crowd parted and stared while the procession of seven men, four boys and a dog—most streaked with coal, one handcuffed—passed through on their way to the entrance. When Tretheway looked back from the front hall, he was surprised to see that, except for one or two people staring after them, the party had resumed.

Tretheway decided that it was unnecessary for him and Jake to accompany everyone downtown. Besides, he realized, there wasn't room. The three Scouts were put in the back seat of the first unmarked police car with two of Wan Ho's men up front. Wan Ho sat in the back of the second car between MacCulla and the NCO Scout. Dr Nooner sat in the passenger seat beside the detective who had played at being bartender.

"You'd better get back to the party," Wan Ho said. "You'll have to mix your own drinks now."

Tretheway nodded.

Wan Ho waved as both cars pulled slowly away from the curb. The NCO Scout had his head in his hands. MacCulla looked neither to the left nor the right. Tretheway watched with Jake as the two cars ran silently over the snow-covered road to the corner, gave two proper hand signals, then turned left and disappeared into the darkness.

Fred nuzzled Tretheway's bare hand.

"Come in from the cold," Addie shouted from the front door. "You'll catch your death."

When Tretheway came downstairs fifteen minutes later, he was clean in looks and smell. His smoking jacket, covered with black smudges and with one sleeve torn half-off, lay where he had dropped it, at the foot of his giant bed. He wore instead a comfortable canary yellow sweatshirt. This one carried the words, "Windsor/Detroit Police Games 1929", with the appropriate city crests.

Controller Joseph Pennylegion was first to approach him. "It was MacCulla, wasn't it?"

Tretheway nodded. He realized for the first time that Pennylegion was a teetotaller.

"He killed all those people," Pennylegion said.

Tretheway wasn't sure, but he thought he detected a hint of admiration in Pennylegion's statement.

"And I never liked him." Pennylegion walked away, shaking his wrinkled brow.

Jake appeared, also clean, but he hadn't changed his sweater. "Did you tell Pennylegion?" he asked Tretheway.

"He guessed."

"Did you tell the others?"

"Not yet."

"Addie won't."

"I know."

Tretheway looked into the sunroom. Bunny Berrigan's record of "I Can't Get Started" was background for what looked like a successful party. About half the people were dancing. The others chatted or drank. Morgan Morgan had taken over as bartender.

"Hate to break up a party," Tretheway said.

"Maybe you won't have to," Jake suggested.

Tretheway went into the party. Jake followed.

"I think everybody's smashed," Jake said.

"God bless Gum's Scouts." Tretheway stopped one as he rushed by carrying an empty glass. "How's the tooth?"

"Tooth?" The Scout ran his tongue along his teeth until it slipped into the space. "Oh. Fine, I guess."

"Keep up the good work." Tretheway let him go. "I think you're right, Jake. Look at the Chief."

"There's something wrong with his eyes."

"He hasn't moved away from there all night."

"Somebody said he fell off his chair at midnight."

Tretheway waved at Zulp. He didn't wave back. Mrs Zulp tried to read Tretheway's sweatshirt.

The Mayor danced by. "Tretheway," he said. "What was that

uniform MacCulla had on? Dammitall. He looked smart." Mrs Trutt backed up her husband's opinion with a quick jerk of her head.

"I'm not really sure," Tretheway said.

"Never mind. I'll ask him tomorrow." They danced away.

At the bar a small group had gathered. Tretheway signalled over their heads to Morgan. Morgan passed over a cold Molson Blue.

"Quite a night," Tretheway said to everyone.

Mrs Pennylegion winked clumsily at Tretheway.

"You're out of uniform," Morgan reprimanded.

One of Pennylegion's men was busily explaining the difference between Win, Place and Show to Gertrude Valentini. Neither noticed Tretheway or Jake.

Gum edged up to Tretheway. "What was all that with Mac?" he whispered.

"You noticed?" Tretheway whispered back.

"Certainly."

"And you're concerned?"

"Of course."

Tretheway decided not to pussyfoot. "MacCulla's the murderer. His Scouts are accessories. They tried to blow us up. House and all. Nitroglycerin. In the cellar. They've all gone to jail."

Bartholomew Gum looked serious. He shifted his weight onto his other foot, started to say something, then went back to looking serious. Finally he shook his index finger under Tretheway's nose. "Never trust a Sea Scout." He bobbed his head once emphatically and turned back to the bar.

"Let's go find Addie," Jake suggested.

"Good idea," Tretheway said. "I need to talk to someone sensible."

On their way to the kitchen, Emmett O'Dell confronted them. "We should be thinking about having a sing."

Tretheway walked by without answering.

"In a few minutes, Emmett," Jake replied.

Emmett started to hum.

They found Addie in the kitchen. She had made two more loaves of sandwiches and was starting a third.

"Addie," Tretheway said. "We don't need any more sandwiches."

"Poor Mac." Addie continued slicing. "What happened to him?"

"I don't know," Tretheway sighed.

"Too much Clausewitz?" Jake asked.

"Something like that. He must've fallen in love with old Germany. Or Prussia."

"Hard to believe his influence over those boys." Addie shook her head.

"I know," Tretheway agreed. "But look what's happening everywhere. In London. Europe. Sometimes I think the whole world's going funny."

O. Pitts pushed through the kitchen door. "I have a question." Tretheway grunted.

"Why was MacCulla dressed up to look like a lion tamer?" O. Pitts piped.

"Leave the kitchen," Addie told him.

The party eventually ran down. Pennylegion and party were the first to go. "You never know," he said to Tretheway on the way out.

The others left, mostly two by two, without learning any more of what had transpired one floor beneath their dancing feet.

"Wait'll they hear the news tomorrow," Tretheway said.

Chief Zulp tried to say something that sounded like "Good Night", but he couldn't manage it. Mrs Zulp drove home. Tretheway found out the next day that it was the first time she had driven a car.

Shortly after four a.m., Tretheway, Jake and Addie watched through the open front door as the last pair, Morgan Morgan and Bartholomew Gum, went down the steps arm in arm. Bartholomew had kindly offered Morgan the spare bedroom at his house to save him the trip home. "But don't wake Mother," he cautioned his new friend.

"Well, that's the last of them," Addie said.

"Who's that?" Jake asked.

Tretheway yanked the door open. Dr Nooner was coming up the steps.

"Just stopped by to tell you everthing's under control." Nooner came inside. "They're all locked up. I gave MacCulla a sedative. Mind you, only after he talked. Of his own free will. He told all."

"He did?" Tretheway said.

"Yes. Wan Ho's got it all down. MacCulla killed them all. Everyone on a different holiday. In a different way. Fascinating.

Just to obscure the real motive. Politics. And according to his hero, Clausewitz . . ."

"War is a mere continuance of political policy by another means," Tretheway interrupted.

"You mean, Mac was at war?" Jake asked.

"With us?" Addie asked.

"Exactly," Dr Nooner continued. "Hitler against Churchill, King George against the Kaiser, Prussia against the world. The good guys against the bad guys. Only in Mac's mind, we were the bad guys. He started out just admiring Germany. Specifically Clausewitz. Then he simply went over the edge."

"An understatement," Jake said.

Addie nodded. "He didn't seem that unstable," she said.

"He fooled us all, Addie," Dr Nooner said. He cocked his head at Tretheway. "I have a feeling that this doesn't surprise you. That you somehow . . . knew."

"Surmised," Tretheway said. "But it's still a shock."

Addie and Jake clucked sympathetically.

"There's one thing," Dr Nooner said. "The nitroglycerin. MacCulla couldn't understand why it didn't explode. And neither can I."

Tretheway smiled smugly.

"Do you know something?"

Tretheway's smile broadened.

"Did you do something to it? Earlier?"

Tretheway nodded. "I added an alkali. To neutralize it."

"What sort of an alkali?"

"Ammonia."

"Where'd you get it?"

"Gertrude Valentini's smelling salts."

There was a pause.

"Where'd you learn your chemistry?" Nooner asked.

"From the Library. One day last week."

There was an uncomfortable silence before Dr Nooner continued. He didn't raise his voice. "It is dangerous to decompose an ester under laboratory conditions with exact measurements and pure chemicals." He pronounced each word distinctly. "And you're telling me that, under primitive conditions in your dusty cellar, armed with knowledge from a library book, you poured Mrs Valentini's lumpy smelling salts into a container of nitroglycerine?"

Jake's eyes looked like an owl's. Addie hadn't blinked for two minutes.

"I shouldn't have?"

"No," Dr Nooner said.

"It could have . . .?"

"Yes." Dr Nooner clasped his hands together, then pulled them apart quickly to mime an explosion. He made an appropriate noise with his mouth.

The second uncomfortable silence was longer than the first.